THE USBORNE BOOK OF GHOSTS & HAUNTINGS

Anna Claybourne

Designed by Stephen Wright, Andrea Slane
and Katherine Smith

Illustrations by Graham Humphreys,
Ian Jackson, Barry Jones and Luis Rey

Managing Designer: Stephen Wright
Edited by Jane Chisholm

Studio photography by Howard Allman and Sue Atkinson
Digital images and textures created by John Russell
Cover design by Stephen Wright and Andrea Slane

Additional designs and digital images created by Zöe Wray
Additional digital images and textures created by Mike Olley
Additional illustrations by Gary Bines, Trevor Boyer, Adrian Chesterman,
Les Edwards, Jeremy Gower, Nicholas Hewetson,
John Russell, Harvey Parker, Lee Stannard and Darrell Warner

With thanks to Tony Allan, Caroline Young, Michèle Busby and Non Figg

CONTENTS

WHAT IS A GHOST?

DO GHOSTS REALLY EXIST? WHY DO WE FIND THEM SO FRIGHTENING? AND WHERE DO GHOST STORIES COME FROM? THIS BOOK CAN HELP YOU FIND OUT.

Do you believe in ghosts? Many people think they have seen a ghost, and even if you never have, you probably know someone who has a spooky ghost story to tell. But what exactly is a ghost, and how do you know when you've spotted one?

In films and stories, ghosts are usually the spirits of dead people, and look like faint versions of them. However, in real life, people claim to see many different types of ghosts ~ human ghosts, animal ghosts and even ghost ships. Some are so solid they look just like the real thing, while others are only a faint glow.

LIVING GHOSTS

It isn't only the dead who appear as ghosts ~ living people may also appear in a ghostly form, far away from where they really are. Some people even claim to have seen their own ghost, known as a Doppelganger.

INVISIBLE GHOSTS

Ghosts are sometimes called "apparitions" ~ which means something that appears. However, not all ghosts can be seen. Poltergeists, for example, are invisible ghosts that throw objects around and make strange banging noises.

DO GHOSTS EXIST?

Whether or not ghosts really exist is a different question ~ and this book doesn't have the answers. Instead, it retells some of the many real-life ghost stories reported by witnesses from around the world. Maybe, after reading these stories, you'll be able to make up your own mind what ghosts really are.

HAUNTED HOUSES

FROM FAMILY HOMES TO ANCIENT CASTLES, ANY TYPE OF HOUSE CAN BE HAUNTED BY THE RESTLESS SPIRITS OF THOSE WHO ONCE LIVED THERE.

The place you're most likely to see a ghost is in a haunted house. Ghosts are usually thought to haunt houses because they cannot rest in their graves. For example, if someone was murdered in the house, and their body was hidden instead of being given a proper funeral, their ghost may try to tell people where the bones can be found. Burying hidden bones like these often seems to put a stop to the haunting.

HAPPY AT HOME

On the other hand, some ghosts just don't seem ready to leave a house they loved when they were alive. Fyvie Castle in Scotland is said to be haunted by a lady who once lived there, Dame Lilies Drummond. She married the owner of the castle, Lord Fyvie, in 1592, and was very happy. Over the next nine years, she had five beautiful daughters. But, sadly, Dame Lilies died young, at the age of 29.

According to gossip, Lord Fyvie was in love with another woman named Lady Grizel Leslie, and poor Dame Lilies had died of a broken heart.

Just six months later, Lord Fyvie married Lady Grizel, and took her home to Fyvie Castle. They spent the night in a small bedroom high up in the castle. But, strangely, they were kept awake by sad, sighing noises which seemed to come from right outside the window. In the morning, they soon found out who it had been. Dame Lilies' name had been carved, upside down, in the stone window ledge. She had come home.

Old, dark houses with turrets and towers may seem scary ~ but any type of house can be haunted.

SIGNS OF A HAUNTED HOUSE

Is there a spook in your street? These are the classic symptoms found in the most famous haunted houses:

• Strange noises ~ including footsteps, thumps, bumps, crashes, and scratching sounds.
• Disembodied voices talking, screaming, moaning, groaning, shouting or laughing.
• Doors and windows that open and shut by themselves.
• A ghost that repeatedly walks through the same part of the house, such as up the staircase, or across a particular room or corridor.
• Blood appearing from nowhere, or bloodstains that can't be cleaned off.
• Animals are disturbed by an invisible presence. Dogs bark at someone no one else can see.

WALKING THROUGH WALLS

In films, cartoons and ghost stories, ghosts frequently walk through walls. But why would they want to?

In fact, the explanation is quite simple. Old houses and castles have often been rebuilt and extended over time. Old doorways are filled in and new walls are built. But a ghost of someone who died long ago would follow the same routes that person used when they were alive ~ ignoring any new walls that have been added.

MORE BUILDINGS

Other buildings besides houses can be haunted too. Many theatres have a resident ghost, such as the one that haunts the Theatre Royal in London, England. He wears a cloak and a large hat, and always walks past the rows of seats and into the wall. There are also haunted pubs, schools and even offices. Houses are most likely to be haunted, though ~ perhaps because people are more likely to die at home.

According to witnesses, the area where a ghost appears often feels icy-cold.

CREEPY CREAKING

A few houses, like the ones described on the following pages, do really seem to be haunted. But remember that many "hauntings" could have a natural explanation. At night, some houses creak as the temperature drops, making the woodwork shrink and move slightly. Central heating pipes can make groaning or tapping noises, and sometimes mice can be heard scampering and scratching. So don't let a few spooky sounds scare you!

GRUESOME GLAMIS CASTLE

THE FOLLOWING PAGES RELATE JUST A FEW OF THE MANY TERRIFYING TALES ASSOCIATED WITH GLAMIS, AN ANCIENT SCOTTISH CASTLE RIDDLED WITH STRANGE SECRETS.

The castles of Scotland, with their thick stone towers, deep dungeons and long history of war, murder and tribal feuds, are often thought to be haunted. The victims of Scotland's violent past may still wander their battlements and winding staircases, desperately searching for rest or revenge.

Yet one castle stands out, not only for its huge number of ghost stories, but for their grisliness and horror. It is the ancestral home of the Earls of Strathmore, set just outside the Tayside village of Glamis (pronounced "glahms").

MYSTERY HISTORY

No one knows exactly how old Glamis Castle is. Large parts of it were built between the seventeenth and nineteenth centuries, making it look more like a large hotel than a crumbling ruin. But at its heart is an ancient solid stone tower, more than a thousand years old, where most of the hauntings are said to take place.

Glamis, one of many Scottish castles, is in the east of Scotland.

Who built this first tower, and exactly when, remains a mystery; but it soon became the scene of a brutal murder. King Malcolm II of Scotland was stabbed to death there in 1034 by a gang of rebels. His blood soaked into the floor, leaving a stain that some say can still be seen to this day ~ even though the floorboards have been replaced.

Glamis Castle looks quite new from the outside, but in the middle is an ancient stone tower where many ghosts, including a phantom knight, have been spotted.

CHALICE CURSE

Glamis Castle belonged to the Scottish royal family until 1372, when King Robert II gave it to his son-in-law, Sir John Lyon. Sir John's home had previously been at Forteviot, near Perth, where he kept a lucky chalice ~ a huge drinking cup which was said to guard the family's good fortune.

Tradition held that if the cup were ever removed from Forteviot, it would bring a curse on the family. But Sir John ignored the warning and took the chalice with him to Glamis.

Bad luck seemed to strike after the Lyon family's chalice was moved to Glamis.

BAD LUCK

Sir John settled into his new home, and for a while he lived there happily. But in 1383, eleven years after he had arrived, he was killed in a deadly duel ~ becoming the first of many of his descendants to meet a violent, sudden or gruesome end at Glamis.

Had the unlucky chalice somehow brought a curse, as promised, on the Lyon family? No one knows ~ but ever since Sir John's death, bad luck, mysterious murders and horrible hauntings have plagued the castle's inhabitants.

THE GREY LADY

One of Glamis's most famous ghost stories dates from 1542, when James V, who was then the King of Scotland, died suddenly. Janet Douglas, wife of the Lord of Glamis, was suspected of murdering him. In those days, belief in witchcraft was widespread, and people accused Janet Douglas of being a witch.

Janet was burned at the stake ~ a terrible and agonizing death ~ and the castle was handed back to the Crown. But a short time later, Janet was proved innocent. Glamis Castle was returned to her family, and ever since, her ghost has been seen regularly. The phantom reputedly haunts the castle chapel and corridors, and has been seen floating above the clock tower in an eerie red glow ~ perhaps to remind visitors of the cruel death she was forced to suffer all those years ago.

These witches were drawn to illustrate Shakespeare's play *Macbeth*. In the play, Macbeth murders King Duncan at Glamis Castle.

THE GAME OF CARDS

Glamis is also said to be haunted by an Earl who once lived there. In 1957, a servant at the castle, Florence Foster, said she had been kept awake at night by an unusual noise. It was the sound of dice being rolled, followed by the shuffling of cards and the voices of two men, swearing and cursing in strange, old-fashioned words.

The noise frightened Florence ~ especially because she knew no one was playing cards anywhere near her room. In fact, she resigned rather than spend another night listening to the ghostly gamblers.

Whose were the strange voices she heard? Were they connected to an old story told about the third Earl of Glamis, who lived in the castle in the late 17th century?

DATE WITH THE DEVIL

Patrick, the third Earl, was a notorious drunkard and gambler whose wild lifestyle was known throughout the land.

Late one Saturday night, he was drinking and playing cards with his friend the Earl of Crawford, in a secret room in the ancient tower. A servant reminded them that the Sabbath was approaching ~ that is, Sunday, when gambling was forbidden.

Patrick rudely replied that he would play cards for as long as he wanted to, and he didn't care if the Devil himself joined in. According to legend, when midnight struck, the Devil appeared. He told both men that they had paid for their card game with their souls. After their deaths, they would be doomed to play on in that same room for eternity.

The story is an old tradition and probably started off as a joke about the third Earl's wicked ways. But perhaps he, like so many of Glamis's ancestors, has stayed behind in spirit to haunt the castle's modern inhabitants.

In the past, many people saw gambling with playing cards as a wicked activity. No one was supposed to play cards on a Sunday.

THE SECRET HEIR

Another story also concerns a secret room. Legend has it that one of the heirs to the castle was born very deformed. His father was afraid people would disapprove and, not wanting anyone to know, he kept the child locked away in a specially built hidden chamber, hoping he would not survive for very long.

However, this rightful heir lived to a great age, and his existence was kept a secret by several generations of Earls. When he finally died, the secret room was bricked up with the body still inside.

It is said that no one has ever found the hidden chamber ~ except once. A workman was said to have been overcome with horror after accidentally stumbling upon a secret room carved deep into the castle's thick walls. No one knows what he saw there, for the terrified man was sworn to secrecy. The castle's owner paid for him and his family to move to Australia soon after.

Whatever horrors the workman saw in the secret room are still waiting to be discovered.

KNIGHT FRIGHT

Several guests at the castle have had sleepless nights. One woman woke to the sound of footsteps rushing up the old spiral staircase. They were followed by a clash of swords, a cry of pain and the gruesome sound of metal slicing into bone. The guest then stared in horror as a pool of blood began to seep through the crack under her door.

The next night she was woken up again, this time by a huge knight leaning over her bed. A few seconds later, he vanished.

A few years later, a couple stayed in the castle with their son. Late one night, they saw a fully armed knight striding into their son's bedroom. The ghost disappeared ~ but the boy said a giant had been bending over his bed.

Two different eyewitness described the ghostly knight looming scarily over their beds.

THE CASTLE TODAY

Glamis Castle is still home to the Lyon family, and is also used as a residence by the British royal family. Thousands of people visit every year ~ probably hoping to catch a glimpse of one of its many ghosts.

AMITYVILLE'S HOUSE OF HORROR

DESPITE ITS NAME ~ WHICH MEANS "FRIENDLY TOWN" ~ THE AMITYVILLE DISTRICT OF LONG ISLAND, U.S.A., IS ASSOCIATED WITH ONE OF THE BEST-KNOWN HAUNTINGS OF ALL TIME. BUT DID IT REALLY HAPPEN...?

Amityville first became famous when a book called *The Amityville Horror*, by Jay Anson, was published in 1978. It claimed to tell the true story of the Lutz family, who said they had been terrorized by ghosts, strange noises and paranormal events when they moved into a house in Ocean Avenue, Amityville, in 1975. By 1979, the book had been made into a film, and the Lutzes were rich. The name Amityville has been linked with horror stories ever since.

A still from the film *Amityville II*, one of three films about the haunting. It shows the house's bedroom windows looking like a pair of huge, staring eyes.

MURDER

The house on Ocean Avenue did have a horrible history. In 1974, a year before the Lutzes moved in, a young man named Ronald DeFeo had murdered his entire family there ~ his mother, father, two sisters and two brothers. Some said DeFeo wanted to get his hands on his parents' money; others said he had gone crazy. Either way, he was sent to prison for life, and the huge house was put up for sale. George and Kathy Lutz were able to buy it for a bargain price of just $80,000.

STENCH AND SLIME

According to *The Amityville Horror*, the trouble began almost as soon as the Lutzes and their three children moved in on December 18. First, the house was filled with a strong, disgusting smell, which seemed to come from nowhere. Then a strange black slime began to appear in the bathroom. It coated the furniture, and could not be removed with any household cleaning products. The Lutzes were even more worried when a huge swarm of flies was found in one of the bedrooms.

SPOOKY VISITOR

It soon became clear that something supernatural was going on. The house's heavy front door was found ripped off its hinges ~ something no human being would have been strong enough to do. Then the Lutzes found strange, hoof-like footprints in the snow outside their house. They led to the garage ~ and the garage door had also been torn open.

INVISIBLE EVIL

Things got even worse as the evil forces in the house seemed to close in on Kathy Lutz. She often felt invisible arms wrapping themselves around her, and painful red marks appeared on her skin. She even began to levitate, or float into the air.

George described how, on January 10, he woke up in the night and couldn't get back to sleep. He turned to Kathy, and was horrified to see her floating at least 30cm (12 inches) above the bed. He grabbed her and pulled her down again. Then, as he watched, his wife's appearance began to change. Her hair went white, wrinkles grew in her face, and her mouth dribbled. She had turned into an old woman. Then, as George stared in horror, she gradually changed back.

TIME TO GO

Finally, ghostly figures started to appear, including a tall hooded figure in a white cloak, and a hideous demon. By January 14, the Lutzes had had enough. They moved out ~ having spent less than a month in their new home.

WAS IT A FAKE?

The huge success of the book about the haunting, and the films that followed, have made Amityville a household name. But, ironically, this is an example of a "real-life" ghost story that in fact seems likely to be a fake.

When investigators tried to discover what really went on at Amityville, they found that the Lutzes had told their story before ~ and it hadn't been the same. For a newspaper article in 1976, George Lutz only described feeling uneasy in the house ~ which was hardly surprising. A year later, the story appeared again, in *Good Housekeeping* magazine. More details had been added, including the part about Kathy becoming an old woman ~ but not about her floating in the air. It wasn't until the book was written in 1978 that tales of levitation were added.

The Lutzes said a ghostly figure cloaked in white had roamed through the house.

SHORT OF CASH

There may be a simple explanation for the "Amityville horror" ~ the Lutzes needed money. The house was cheap, but it still cost more than they could really afford. They may have sensed a scary presence in the house ~ but they may also have exaggerated their fears into a full-blown ghost story in order to get out of debt.

THE RIDDLE OF BORLEY RECTORY

WAS BORLEY RECTORY REALLY THE MOST HAUNTED HOUSE IN ENGLAND? THREE FAMILIES AND A FAMOUS INVESTIGATOR BORE WITNESS TO GHOSTLY GOINGS-ON AT THE HOUSE - BUT COULD IT ALL HAVE BEEN A CUNNING HOAX?

I n 1862, the Reverend Henry Bull arrived in the village of Borley, England, to take up his post as the new parson. As soon as he had settled in, he decided to build a new rectory by the church for his family to live in.

The house was completed in 1863, despite gossip that it was built on haunted land. The site was once occupied by a monastery where, it was said, a nun had been put to death for having an affair with a monk.

This photograph of Borley Rectory shows the gates where the phantom nun was sometimes seen.

As well as appearing in the rectory garden and outside the gates, the nun's ghost often stared in gloomily through the windows of the house.

NOSY NUN

As soon as the family moved in, strange things started to happen. One of Bull's daughters was often disturbed by footsteps outside her room, and the sound of someone knocking three times. But no one was there.

Other members of the family heard odd noises and saw shadowy figures. But the most frequent visitor was the ghost of a nun. She often wandered across the garden, along a path that soon became known as Nun's Walk. She also scared the family by peering in at them through the windows.

Henry Bull didn't mind the nun at first. He even had a summer house built in the garden so that he could sit and watch her. But after a while he had the dining-room window bricked up, because the nun kept staring through it while members of the family were having their meals.

GLOOMY GHOST

In 1892 Henry Bull died and his son Harry took over. The family stayed in the rectory, and in 1900 three of Harry's sisters had an even closer encounter with the nun's unhappy ghost.

Two of the girls were coming home from a party one night, when they saw a female figure dressed in a long black habit. It was gliding across the lawn, and they knew it was the phantom nun. One of the girls ran inside to get their sister Elizabeth, who was not convinced by the haunting. She marched into the garden, declaring that her sisters' talk of a ghost was "nonsense". She strode toward the figure, which stopped moving. It faced the girls with an expression of intense grief, then vanished.

CREEPY COACH

During this time, the area around Borley Rectory was also frequently haunted by a phantom horse-drawn carriage, which rattled along the nearby lane. According to some witnesses, the carriage glowed with a strange light as it sped past the rectory and into the darkness.

Harry Bull claimed that when he was in the lane, he often heard the rumbling of the wheels and the jangling of the horses' bridles, but never actually managed to catch a glimpse of the coach itself.

However, a gardener at the rectory claimed he had seen it several times, charging at high speed along the lane before disappearing as it reached a nearby farm. On one moonlit night, he watched the phantom carriage for over 30 seconds before it vanished.

This plan of Borley Rectory's grounds shows where the phantom coach and nun were seen.

NO REST

The Bull family finally left the house in 1927, after Harry Bull died. But the haunting continued to plague the new residents. First came the Reverend Eric Smith and his wife.

The Smiths didn't believe in ghosts and weren't afraid, but they soon realized that something strange was happening. As well as hearing footsteps and unexplained noises, they saw keys throwing themselves out of keyholes, and dishes flung to the floor by an unseen hand. And their servants claimed to have seen the nun and the phantom coach.

Keys left in keyholes in the haunted rectory often jumped out onto the floor.

INVESTIGATION

The Smiths wrote to a newspaper, the *Daily Mirror*, about what was going on, and the paper sent a ghost hunter, Harry Price, to investigate the haunting. When he arrived, chaos broke out. More keys jumped out of their keyholes, bricks sailed through the air and a candlestick flew down the stairs. Price reported it all to the *Daily Mirror*, the case became a national news story and tourists flocked to see the house. Eventually, the pressure was so great that the Smiths moved out.

Harry Price's investigation of Borley Rectory made him famous. He wrote about the case in his book *Search for the Truth*, published in 1942.

MARIANNE

The new parson was the Reverend Lionel Foyster. He moved in in 1930 with his young family and his wife Marianne, who seemed to inspire even stranger and scarier events.

At first, the haunting was the same as before. Reverend Foyster decided to keep a record of anything unusual, and he noted down hundreds of mysterious noises, moving objects and other paranormal happenings.

Up until now, the haunting at Borley had been mostly harmless. But after the Foysters moved in, the ghosts gradually became more violent, and began picking on Marianne. She was slapped by an invisible hand and dragged out of her bed during the night. Scariest of all, messages to her began to appear on one of the walls inside the house, written in crooked, childlike handwriting. One simply said: "Marianne, please help get".

Spooky messages like this one began to appear on the walls of Borley Rectory. No one knew how they got there.

FISHY FOYSTERS?

Marianne decided the spirit that was speaking to her belonged to a young Catholic woman ~ possibly a nun. Once she asked the girl's spirit what it wanted. The sad reply the ghost gave was "Rest..."

But Harry Price noticed that there were far fewer signs of the supernatural when Marianne wasn't around. This could have been because she was a "focus" for a poltergeist (see page 24). However, Price thought she could have been faking some of the things that happened to her.

Eventually, after five years, the Foysters too moved out. The house had gained such a reputation that the next clergyman to arrive in Borley didn't want to live there, and the haunted rectory lay empty.

BOFFINS MOVE IN

No one lived in Borley Rectory until 1937, when Harry Price himself decided to rent it. He arranged for dozens of volunteers to stay in the house and record any strange happenings.

The team noted many spooky events, but their best results came from a seance they held. Using a pointer called a planchette to spell out words, they began to receive messages from the spirit of a nun named Marie Lairre. She said a local landowner had abducted her from her nearby convent in 1667 and strangled her. She also predicted that the rectory would burn down that night, and that her bones would be found in the ruins.

BORLEY BONFIRE

The prediction did come true, but not until 11 months later, when a man named Captain Gregson bought the house. As he was moving in, an oil lamp fell over in the hall. The whole building burned to the ground.

In 1943 Harry Price returned to the ruins to search for the nun's bones. Digging under the cellar floor, he unearthed a jawbone and part of a skull. Experts found they were those of a woman aged about 30.

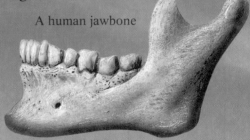
A human jawbone

But although Price had the bones buried, the nun was still not at rest. A doctor saw her by the rectory gates in 1949, and sightings are still reported to this day.

HOAXER HARRY?

Borley Rectory certainly seems to deserve its title "the most haunted house in England". Many people claimed they saw and heard supernatural phenomena while they were there.

Yet some experts think Harry Price himself faked the ghosts. Perhaps he wanted the house to look haunted so he could gain fame and fortune from the story. Whatever the truth, Price took it with him to his grave, and Borley's spooky reputation remains.

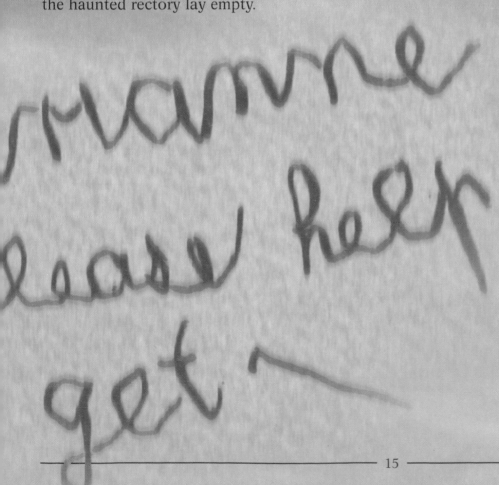

THE WINCHESTER MYSTERY MANSION

SARAH WINCHESTER WAS SO AFFECTED BY THE GHOSTS HAUNTING HER THAT SHE BUILT A HOUSE FOR THEM! BY THE TIME SHE DIED, HER HAUNTED MANSION WAS THE WEIRDEST HOUSE IN THE WORLD.

When Sarah Pardee got married in 1862, she knew she would never have to worry about money. Her husband was William Winchester, the heir to a huge fortune. His family had made their wealth manufacturing guns, including the Winchester Rifle, known as "the Gun that Won the West". It had been used to kill thousands of people in the many battles for land and power on the Western frontier.

Sarah Winchester

SAD STORY

The couple's wealth, however, did not bring them happiness. Sarah had a baby, but it died at just a few weeks old. Then, in 1881, her husband William died of tuberculosis. Sarah was left alone and heartbroken, at the age of 40, with no family and so much money she hardly knew what to do with it.

In those days, Spiritualism was all the rage. Spiritualists believed that the dead could contact the living, with the help of a person called a medium. Hoping to hear from her dear husband and child, Sarah went to a medium for advice.

VENGEFUL VICTIMS

But Sarah was in for a shock. Instead of her loved ones, the medium brought news of other spirits ~ the souls of the many victims of the Winchester rifle. They were haunting Sarah, the medium explained, and had actually caused the deaths in her family. And it seemed there was only one way to stop them.

The solution, according to the medium, was to build a home for all the spirits ~ and to keep on improving it. No one knows why this was supposed to help, but Sarah Winchester certainly took the advice to heart.

BUILDING BEGINS

A couple of years later, Sarah bought a house in San José, California. It was not a large home ~ just a simple eight-room farmstead. But, from then on, she employed builders and carpenters 24 hours a day, seven days a week, to extend and modify the house to her specifications.

In all, Sarah added over 700 new rooms to the house. At one time it had seven floors and was topped with towers and turrets, but some of these were destroyed in a huge earthquake in 1906. Sarah also kept having rooms demolished and replaced over the years to keep the builders busy.

A postcard showing an aerial view of the Winchester House.

Greetings from WINCHESTER MYSTERY HOUSE

LABYRINTH

The house is now known as the Winchester Mystery House. It has 160 rooms spread over four floors, 467 doors and over 1,000 windows. But the Winchester Mystery House is not just big ~ it is also very strange.

The modifications include spooky staircases that lead nowhere, secret passageways and tunnels, and doors that open into thin air or onto walls. Some rooms have no door at all. There is even a chimney that rises four floors, only to end just below the ceiling.

This staircase goes nowhere ~ just straight into the back of a cupboard.

This door is tiny, but Sarah Winchester was so small she could fit through it.

Slats were added to prevent tourists falling out of this crazy midair door.

This airshaft ends just under a skylight ~ so it can't let any air in!

LOOPY LIFESTYLE

While she was alive, Sarah herself behaved very oddly as well. Locals said she slept in a different bedroom every night, and in the evenings held mysterious meetings with the spirits that were haunting her. She even threw banquets for them, sitting down at the stroke of midnight at a table set for 13 people ~ but the servants could only see Sarah sitting there by herself.

NEW IDEAS

Did the spirits tell Sarah what to build? Or did she make the house complicated to confuse them? Either way, she came up with some useful inventions, such as push-button switches for lights, which are still used today.

The Winchester Mystery House is now one of California's biggest tourist attractions, and some say it is still haunted. Guided tours are held every day ~ and also at midnight on every Friday the 13th and Halloween.

SOLDIERS IN THE CELLAR

THIS GHOSTLY ROMAN ARMY, SPOTTED IN THE CELLAR OF AN OLD HOUSE, COULD BE AN EXAMPLE OF A "CYCLICAL" HAUNTING. CYCLICAL GHOSTS BLINDLY REPEAT ACTIONS FROM THEIR OWN LIFETIMES, HARDLY NOTICING THOSE WHO WITNESS THEM.

The Treasurer's House is a large, grand building near the middle of the ancient city of York, England. There have been several ghostly reports about the house, but they weren't all gathered together until 1974, when a plumber named Harry Martindale made public what he had seen while he was working there in 1953.

The Treasurer's House in York, England

ALONE IN THE CELLAR

Harry was fitting central heating in the house's cellar when he noticed an odd noise. It seemed to come from inside the walls, but he assumed it must be a radio upstairs, and went on working. The sound grew louder, and suddenly a man's head, wearing a helmet and blowing a trumpet, emerged from the wall right next to Harry. He was so shocked he fell off the small ladder he was standing on. Then he hurried into a corner and hid there, watching in amazement.

ROMAN REGIMENT

The trumpeter's whole body appeared, and was followed by a large carthorse. Then more men, all dressed in Roman military uniform, marched out of the wall and across the cellar. Harry realized that the sound the trumpet made was the sound he had heard coming from the walls earlier.

The Roman soldiers were carrying heavy swords and large round shields.

NO FEET

Harry noticed that the Romans' legs seemed to disappear into the floor ~ he could only see them from the knees up. As they marched across the room and dissolved into the opposite wall, they went past a hole in the floor, and Harry saw their feet for a moment.

The soldiers didn't notice Harry, and he watched them for some time. They all carried round shields, spears, swords and daggers. They looked tired, as if they were on a long march or returning from a battle. Harry also thought they looked amazingly solid and real, though the way they walked through the walls told him that they must be ghosts.

NO SURPRISE

When the last soldier had disappeared and the sound of the trumpet had died away, Harry ran upstairs to tell someone what he had seen. He found the curator of the museum that was housed in the Treasurer's House. But before he even had time to begin, the curator guessed from Harry's face what had happened. "You've seen the Romans, haven't you?" he said.

Harry recognized the soldiers as Romans by their battle gear.

It turned out that Harry wasn't the first witness to see the spooky soldiers. The curator suggested he should write down what he had seen. When he had finished, the curator showed him two other accounts, written by other visitors who had seen the ghosts. Their descriptions all matched.

But, strangely, the curator had never spread the word about the ghosts in the cellar. Perhaps he didn't want the Treasurer's House to be disturbed by news reporters and investigators. It wasn't until much later, when the story of Harry's experience came out, that other witnesses revealed in public that they had seen the Romans too.

This is the cellar room of the Treasurer's House, where plumber Harry Martindale and several other witnesses claim to have seen a regiment of ghostly Roman soldiers on the march.

"I SAW THEM TOO"

Joan Mawson was the next witness to come forward. She was a caretaker who had worked at the Treasurer's House many years before. One Sunday evening in 1957, she had gone down into the cellar to check the boiler. She took her bull terrier dog with her, but as they approached the cellar the dog started to howl and ran back upstairs.

In the narrow corridor, Joan thought she could hear the sound of horses' hooves. She turned around ~ and was terrified to see a group of Roman soldiers on horseback looming over her. She was afraid the horses would trample her, and she flattened herself against the wall. But neither the soldiers nor their horses seemed to see her at all.

Joan saw the Romans twice more. On one occasion, they were filthy and splattered with mud. The last time she saw them, they looked very tired and were slumped over the necks of their horses.

PARTY PUZZLE

Another story tells of a party held at Treasurer's House in the 1920s by a man named Frank Green. One of the guests went into the cellar, perhaps in a game of hide-and-seek. As she tried to go through a doorway, the guest suddenly found her way was barred by a strange figure, dressed as a Roman soldier. But there was no one at the party dressed as a soldier.

MATCHING REPORTS

It seemed that the witnesses had all seen the same figures, but in different situations ~ on horseback, on foot, and worn out from fighting or marching. It was as if the soldiers had passed that way many times, and their different activities had somehow been "recorded" into their surroundings.

WHO WERE THEY?

York was an important city in Roman times, when it was called Eboracum. Soldiers would have gathered there, marching up and down the Roman roads. It seemed that the Treasurer's House was built on the site of one of these early roads. In 1954 an archaeologist, Peter Wenham, excavated the cellar to look for ruins. He found a Roman road, the Via Decumana, beneath the cellar floor. The hole where Harry had seen the soldiers' feet reached down just as far as the original road surface.

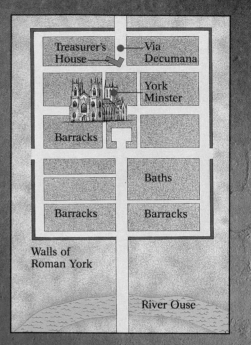

This map shows the layout of the old Roman roads in the part of York around the Treasurer's House.

SHIELD MYSTERY

One puzzle remained ~ the round shields which Harry had seen the soldiers carrying. The Roman soldiers at York, called legionaries, had square shields, not round ones. This made some people think Harry had made up his story.

However, it turned out that for part of the second century AD, the Roman army was split into two sections. Legionaries used square shields, but another regiment, called the auxiliaries, carried round ones. Were they the ghostly soldiers Harry saw?

Roman legionaries usually carried large rectangular shields like this one, while the auxiliary soldiers' shields were round.

THE WALSINGHAM HAUNTING

THE GHOSTS THAT PLAGUED THE WALSINGHAM FAMILY'S HOME IN GEORGIA, U.S.A., IN 1891 DID EVERYTHING THEY COULD TO SCARE MR WALSINGHAM, HIS CHILDREN AND EVEN HIS PETS.

When the Walsingham family moved into a new house in Georgia, U.S.A., none of them believed in ghosts. But the things that happened to them there were to change their minds forever.

LOUD LAUGHTER

The trouble started in 1891, when the Walsinghams began to hear noises at night. At first they thought the screaming and laughing must be coming from next door. But as the wailing grew louder and the laughter grew more evil, they began to get scared. The family dog often barked at a strange presence, and once he was grabbed by a mysterious force and thrown to the ground. The cat, meanwhile, had his fur stroked by an invisible hand.

SHOULDER SHOCK

One night, the youngest girl was sitting in front of a mirror when she felt a touch on her shoulder. Turning around, she saw a ghostly hand lying there. But there was no reflection of the ghost in the mirror. She screamed, and the hand vanished. Meanwhile, Mr. Walsingham was followed by an invisible ghost. He saw its footprints on the ground beside him.

DINNER DISASTER

The last straw came when a dinner party at the Walsingham house turned into a nightmare. As the guests sat around the table, they heard a loud groan from upstairs. Then blood began to drip from the ceiling onto the tablecloth.

Nothing was found in the room above, or anywhere in the house, to explain the drops of blood. But by this time the Walsinghams had had enough. They moved out immediately.

The hand that had touched the girl's shoulder grabbed Horace Gunn around the neck.

FRIGHTFUL FACE

The house stood empty, until a man named Horace Gunn decided to spend a night there to investigate. He fell asleep easily, but later he woke with a start. Floating above him was a disembodied human head, dripping with blood and with an ugly, ghoulish expression.

Gunn was so scared, he couldn't scream. He stumbled out of bed and into the hall. But as he ran, he felt an icy cold, invisible hand grabbing his throat. He fainted, and lay in the hall until the next day.

This experience haunted Gunn for life. But from that day on, the Walsingham ghosts were gone for good.

WHAT CAUSES GHOSTS?

MANY EYEWITNESSES ARE CERTAIN THEY HAVE SEEN A GHOST. YET NO ONE KNOWS WHAT MAKES A GHOST APPEAR, OR WHY SOME PEOPLE SEE THEM AND OTHERS DON'T. ARE GHOSTS REALLY DEAD SPIRITS - OR CAN THEY BE SCIENTIFICALLY EXPLAINED?

The typical ghost in a spooky story is a faint, floating spirit, come to visit the living with a message or a warning. In fact, people report seeing many different types of ghosts ~ some speak, some don't; some look solid and some are see-through; some are scarier than others. Not surprisingly, there are many theories about what causes them.

This "ghost" appeared at a seance held by a medium to contact the dead. Does it look like a ghost to you ~ or could it be someone dressed up?

SPIRITS

Ghosts often seem to be the spirits of dead people. Lord Tyrone's ghost, for example, is said to have visited his sister (see page 44), and two-year-old Greg Maxwell was sure his dead great-grandma was in the room (see page 61). Spiritualism is based on the idea that the dead exist in another world, which we can contact with the help of a medium ~ a person with the ability to speak to spirits. But, if this is true, why aren't we always in touch with the world of the dead? Instead, we just seem to catch tiny glimpses of it. And mediums usually make money from their skills ~ so a lot of them may be fakes.

TAPE RECORDINGS

The "tape recording" theory is sometimes used to explain ghosts such as the Romans in the cellar (see page 18). This theory suggests that our surroundings can somehow "record" events and then play them back like a video ~ which appears as a ghost. These "cyclical ghosts" appear again and again. They seem not to notice the people who see them. Often, they get fainter as time goes on ~ like a tape recording wearing out.

The trouble with this theory is that no one knows how it works. Most video and sound recordings are made by arranging magnetic particles on a tape, or by storing digital information on a CD or disk. Some scientists, such as Don Robins (see page 73) think that natural substances such as quartz can hold digital code, just like a CD. But that doesn't explain why the ghost "video" sometimes plays back and sometimes doesn't.

Amethyst, a type of quartz

If you're on your own at night, it's easy to imagine your house is haunted ~ even if it isn't.

DREAMS

Why do so many ghosts appear at night? There could be a simple explanation ~ dreams. They can seem very real, especially when you've just woken up. For example, the ghost that Lord Lyttelton saw (see page 42) could have been a dream ~ he was the only witness, and it appeared at night in his bedroom. Many people are afraid of the dark and are more likely to feel scared at night. Combined with a very vivid dream, this could make them imagine they have seen a ghost ~ when in fact they haven't at all.

PARANORMAL PUZZLE

Despite all our knowledge, scientists still don't really understand how the human brain works. Whether we imagine ghosts ~ or whether our brains somehow help to create them ~ is still a puzzle. And no one has been able to prove that ghosts *don't* exist. So, until we know more about what ghosts and hauntings really are, people will continue to be scared by them and fascinated by their strangeness.

POLTERGEISTS

POLTERGEISTS ARE AMONG THE MOST COMMON OF ALL PARANORMAL PHENOMENA. BUT ARE THEY REALLY A TYPE OF GHOST, OR A STRANGE CREATION OF THE HUMAN MIND?

The word poltergeist is German for "noisy ghost". In most poltergeist hauntings, there are loud knocking or scratching noises, and objects move by themselves. The "ghost" is usually invisible, but apparitions have been known to appear in some cases. However, some experts think that, despite their strangeness, many poltergeists are not really ghosts at all.

FINDING A FOCUS

While most ghosts seem to be connected with spooky places, such as haunted houses or lonely graveyards, a poltergeist usually attaches itself to a particular person instead. This person is known as the focus. The majority of focuses are girls aged between 11 and 18, although boys and adults have been known to have poltergeists as well.

No one is sure why poltergeists seem to like haunting teenagers so much, but ghost investigators have noticed that focuses are usually people who are very stressed or moody. Some experts have suggested that teenage girls are the most likely people to have strong emotions of this sort. This might explain why they are often found at the heart of poltergeist cases.

FAMOUS CASES

There are dozens of well-documented poltergeist cases. They come from many periods in history and from all over the world ~ but they often have many details in common.

A poltergeist which haunted a house in Enfield, England, in 1977 was a typical example. It seemed to focus on 11-year-old Janet, one of four children in the house. She was thrown out of her bed, and a deep, scary voice spoke out of her mouth. On several occasions, she even found herself floating into the air. Meanwhile, furniture moved around by itself and objects were hurled across rooms. Some objects even seemed to move through solid walls.

Poltergeists are also famous for starting fires, although they are usually small and harmless ones. In Ramos, Brazil, a 13-year-old girl named Sara dreamed that a demon was trying to burn her.

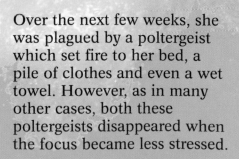

In Sara's dream, a demon threatened to burn her. After she woke up, fires began to start by themselves in her house.

Over the next few weeks, she was plagued by a poltergeist which set fire to her bed, a pile of clothes and even a wet towel. However, as in many other cases, both these poltergeists disappeared when the focus became less stressed.

CAMERA-SHY

Despite being so common, poltergeist hauntings are difficult to record on film. When there's a poltergeist around, cameras, video recorders and even tape recorders often seem to malfunction.

This seems to suggest that many poltergeists are faked. But it's possible that they are caused by a mysterious type of energy, which can affect electrical equipment and stop it from working.

Poltergeists seem to like bricks and stones, and are often reported to throw them around.

Few photos have been taken of poltergeist acitivity, and those that have could have been faked ~ for example by throwing a chair across a room.

MIND POWER

Some experts think poltergeists could actually be caused by energy from people's minds. So far, no one knows how this works, but it could explain why poltergeists affect stressed, anxious people. If they suppress their bad feelings, their worries could come out as a powerful force which makes objects move.

Experts call this force Recurrent Spontaneous Psychokinesis, or RSPK. PK, or psychokinesis, means "mind movement". Some people, such as the psychic Uri Geller, seem to be able to use PK deliberately to move objects. Perhaps focuses create poltergeists using a similar force, but without realizing it.

Most poltergeists seem to focus on anxious or stressed children or teenagers.

GHOSTS

On the other hand, perhaps poltergeists really are ghosts. Sometimes they even claim to be the spirit of a dead person. For example, in 1848, in Hydesville, U.S.A., a house was haunted by shaking and banging noises. Then, using a special code invented by the family, the ghost spelled out a message that it was a spirit of a man whose body was buried beneath the floorboards ~ and indeed human bones were later found there.

Four classic poltergeist tales are told on the following pages. They may help you make up your mind what poltergeists really are...

SPOT A POLTERGEIST

If a haunting features these spooky signs, it's probably a poltergeist:

• Knocking, banging, and animal-like scratching are the first signs of a poltergeist.
• Objects may shuffle, shake, float in the air or fly across rooms.
• Poltergeists often focus on one person. Strange things seem to happen only when the focus is nearby. She may be slapped, bitten, or dragged out of bed.
• Objects may disappear from one place and appear in another.
• Flowers, bricks, sweets and other objects may appear out of thin air. These are called apports.
• Small fires often break out, but cause very little damage.
• The voice of the ghost may be heard rudely insulting its victims.
• A ghostly or monstrous figure may appear ~ especially at the end of the haunting.

THE TEDWORTH DRUMMER

THIS HAUNTING AT AN ENGLISH COUNTRY HOUSE IN 1662 WAS THE FIRST POLTERGEIST TO BE RECORDED IN DETAIL. AT THE TIME IT WAS BLAMED ON WITCHCRAFT, BUT IT BEARS A REMARKABLE SIMILARITY TO MANY MODERN POLTERGEISTS.

For many centuries, most people in Europe and America believed in witchcraft. It was a crime for which both men and women could be tried by law. So when John Mompesson, a respected magistrate, became the victim of a spooky haunting, everyone assumed a witch or wizard must be to blame.

NOISE NUISANCE

The trouble began one day in 1662. Mompesson was at work at the courthouse when he was bothered by a drumming noise outside. It turned out to be coming from a wandering musician named William Drury, who had been hanging around the town for several days, banging a drum and making a nuisance of himself.

Mompesson immediately had Drury brought into the courthouse and ordered him to explain himself. The drummer claimed to have a permit allowing him to perform in the street, but Mompesson investigated and found the permit was a fake. He had Drury arrested and thrown into prison, and confiscated his drum.

STRANGE SOUNDS

Drury was released later that day, but his drum was not returned. Instead, Mompesson took it home to his house in Tedworth, and left it there while he went away to London for two weeks on business.

When he got back he found his family in turmoil. His pregnant wife, young children and servants had all been kept awake at night by banging and knocking noises. They were sure someone was trying to break in ~ but whenever they looked, no one was there.

BEAT OF A DRUM

The trouble continued, and Mompesson and his family noticed a pattern. Most evenings, the noises began at around bedtime with a strange whirring sound. This would change to banging and thumping, and finally to the sound of a drum being played. Each night, after two hours, the noise stopped. This would happen for five nights in a row. After a few nights' break, it would start again.

This picture shows the witchfinder general, Matthew Hopkins. In the 17th-century, professional witchfinders were paid to catch suspected witches and have them tried in court.

The haunting seemed to stop complctcly when Mrs Mompesson had her baby. It seemed as if the ghost meant the newborn child no harm. But a few weeks later it was back ~ with a brand-new bag of tricks.

HAUNTED DAUGHTERS

The disturbance now seemed to "focus" on Mompesson's two daughters, aged 11 and 7. It moved to the room where the two girls slept ~ and it was no longer just a noise. The girls' beds began to shake violently, and sometimes even floated into the air. Mompesson decided to move the girls to an attic room, but the ghost just followed.

MORE WITNESSES

The family thought a priest might be able to help ~ but when he arrived, things got even worse. Chairs walked around, shoes jumped into the air, and the priest was hit on the leg by a flying plank.

News of the ghost, which was now known as the "Tedworth Drummer", spread far and wide. Soon dozens of tourists arrived, hoping to see the spooky events for themselves ~ the King even sent a servant to Tedworth to report on the ghost. One of the visitors, a young clergyman named Joseph Glanvill, wanted to make a written description of the haunting, and was invited to stay overnight.

This engraving, from a 1681 account of the Tedworth haunting, shows John Mompesson's home being plagued by a host of evil spirits.

NIGHT OF FEAR

Glanvill witnessed the banging noises and moving objects in the girls' room. He tried to track down the source of the noise, making sure the girls kept their hands still on the counterpane so it could not be them. But every time he got close, the noise moved to another part of the room.

The ghost didn't seem to welcome Glanvill's investigation, as it soon began to persecute him as well. During the night, he was woken up by a loud knock on his bedroom door ~ but no one was there. When he went to fetch his horse in the morning, he found it sweating and exhausted ~ as if it had been ridden all night. It managed to carry him home, but died mysteriously just a couple of days later.

DRURY'S BOAST

The family suspected that William Drury, the musician whose drum Mompesson had taken, had something to do with the haunting. Then news came that Drury had been put in prison again, this time for stealing pigs. He was said to have boasted to a fellow prisoner that he had bewitched Mompesson, to pay him back for confiscating the drum. So when Drury was sentenced to be deported (sent away) to America, the Mompessons were sure the trouble would stop. But Drury escaped, and the haunting began again. Now, they were sure he was to blame.

PHANTOM FIGURE

The ghost at the Mompessons' house now seemed to develop a more physical presence. First it began to speak: a loud voice could often be heard shouting "A witch! A witch!" in the girls' bedroom. John Mompesson also glimpsed a shadowy figure on the stairs, and one of the servants woke in the night to see a human shape, with glowing red eyes, looming over his bed.

On another occasion, Mompesson was sitting in a downstairs room when he noticed some logs in the fireplace seeming to move by themselves. He immediately drew his pistol and fired in the direction of the logs. Not long afterwards, he found drops of fresh blood on the hearth.

A strange, ghostly figure terrified a servant by looming over him in the night.

GONE AT LAST

The way the troubles ended suggested William Drury had indeed been behind them. Following his mysterious claims he was arrested on charges of witchcraft. Although he was let off ~ perhaps because there was not enough hard evidence to convict him ~ he was still sentenced to be deported for his earlier crime.

In 1663 he left for America ~ and the haunting stopped. This made the Mompessons more convinced than ever that he had been using witchcraft to frighten them ~ a view which was considered quite normal for the time. However, most modern experts on the paranormal say that the spooky events at Tedworth were more likely to have been caused by a poltergeist.

Because the case took place so long ago, no one can find out what really caused it. But there were so many witnesses that the case of the Tedworth Drummer remains one of the most convincing hauntings in history.

This illustration shows a man suspected of witchcraft being tortured to make him confess.

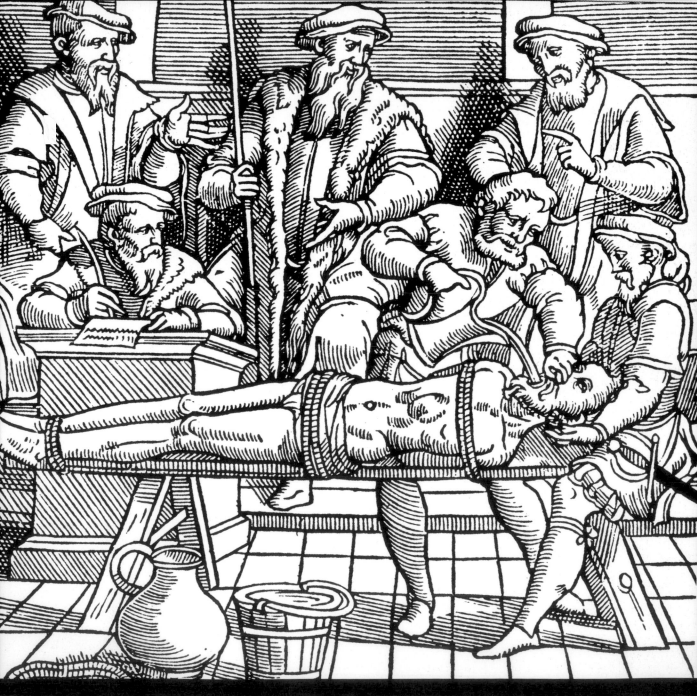

THE PONTEFRACT POLTERGEIST

THIS TROUBLESOME POLTERGEIST WAS REPORTED IN PONTEFRACT, ENGLAND, IN THE 1960S. IT WAS ONE OF THE MOST DRAMATIC AND DETAILED HAUNTINGS EVER - AND THE GHOST EVEN SEEMED TO HAVE A SENSE OF FUN AS WELL.

The Pontefract poltergeist haunted the home of Joe and Jean Pritchard and their two children: Phillip, who was 15, and 12-year-old Diane. But when it made its first appearance, in September 1966, most of the family was away on a trip. Only Phillip was there, along with his grandmother Mrs. Scholes, Jean's mother.

PECULIAR POWDER

On the evening of September 1, Mrs. Scholes was knitting in the living room. Just as Phillip walked in, there was a gust of wind, the back door slammed, and the room suddenly felt icy cold. Then Phillip noticed a cloud of whitish dust, like chalk dust. It hadn't come off the ceiling, as it was only in the lower half of the room. As he watched, it coated the furniture with a thin layer of powder.

Phillip and his grandmother fetched Aunt Marie, who lived across the road. As soon as she walked in, she slipped on a pool of water. They mopped it up, but more appeared. No one ~ not even a man from the water company ~ could figure out where it was coming from.

WALKING WARDROBE

At first, the Pritchards weren't scared, just puzzled. They only realized the house might be haunted when a wardrobe began to sway from side to side and moved across the floor by itself. At that point, Phillip and his grandmother packed their bags and went to stay with Marie.

Later that night, Marie and her husband Vic decided to investigate. They had a friend, Mr. O'Donald, who was interested in ghosts, so they asked him to come and explore the "haunted house".

SPOOKY RESPONSE

As they opened the door, they felt a blast of cold air, but found nothing else unusual. Mr. O'Donald said he thought the problem might be a poltergeist. He added that poltergeists often damaged photographs. Then, as it was quite late, he went home. The moment he had gone, Vic and Marie heard a crash. In the next room, they found the Pritchard's wedding photo on the floor. The glass was broken, and the paper was slashed in two.

THE GHOST IS GONE

After that, the haunting ended, as quickly as it had begun. When the rest of the family returned from their trip, everything was back to normal, and nothing spooky happened in the Pritchard household for two whole years.

Then, one day, Jean Pritchard and Mrs. Scholes were having tea when they heard a noise in the hall. They found the covers from Jean's bed lying at the foot of the stairs. Phillip's bedclothes were thrown downstairs too, along with some potted plants. Mrs. Scholes was sure it was the ghost. "I told you," she said, "it's starting again!"

RETURN VISIT

This time, however, the haunting was much worse than before. The whole house was filled with banging noises and thumps, and the rooms would suddenly become mysteriously cold. Dozens of objects began moving around by themselves.

One of the upstairs rooms in the house was being decorated, and several paintbrushes, a carpet sweeper and a roll of wallpaper were hurled through the air. The kitchen was affected too ~ giant bite marks appeared in a sandwich in the refrigerator.

The Pritchards' priest was horrified to see a candle floating into the air and waving itself under his nose.

HOLY HORROR

Eventually, the Pritchards had had enough. They decided to call in a priest to perform an exorcism ~ a type of religious ceremony which some people think can get rid of ghosts and demons.

When the priest arrived, he suggested that the bumping noises and moving furniture weren't caused by a ghost at all, but by the house subsiding (sinking into the ground). However, he soon changed his mind when, just as he finished speaking, a candlestick floated into the air and waved itself under his nose. Terrified, he left in a hurry, saying there was evil in the house.

A NEW FOCUS

Diane Pritchard, who was now 14, seemed to be the focus of the haunting. This suggested a poltergeist *was* to blame, as they are known to victimize teenagers. Diane was thrown out of bed during the night, and even dragged up the stairs by a pair of invisible hands which grabbed hold of her cardigan.

Diane was tormented by what felt like invisible hands, pushing her, slapping her and dragging her out of bed and up staircases.

However, another family member, Joe Pritchard's no-nonsense sister Maude, didn't believe a word of the stories she heard about a poltergeist at the Pritchards' house. She was sure Diane and Phillip were playing tricks, hoaxing the haunting to get attention.

Convinced she would uncover a fraud, Maude decided to come and visit the Pritchards in Pontefract, in order to see the events for herself.

MAYHEM FOR MAUDE

As soon as Aunt Maude arrived, the lights went out. Then the refrigerator door opened and a jug of milk floated out, crossed the room and poured itself onto Maude's head! Still convinced it was a trick, she decided to stay the night. She and Jean arranged to sleep in the same room as Diane, to keep her company.

That night, the poltergeist put on its most impressive show so far. Food from the refrigerator was strewn all over the kitchen floor, all the lights in the house flickered on and off, and when Maude climbed into bed, her reading lamp detatched itself from the wall and sailed out of the bedroom door. And four tiny lightbulbs, which were part of the gas fire in the living room, materialized in Diane's bedroom.

But the scariest part was yet to come.

When the bedside light flew across the room, Maude had to admit that something very strange was going on.

HAIRY HANDS

Suddenly, an enormous pair of furry hands reached around the door, one at the top and one near the bottom. It looked as if there was a huge monster behind the door ~ until they realized that the hands were in fact Aunt Maude's fur gloves, moving by themselves.

"Get away ~ you're evil!" screamed Aunt Maude. In reply, one of the gloves beckoned the women to come nearer ~ but they were too scared to move. Then Aunt Maude sang a hymn to scare the ghost away, but the gloves merely beat time to the tune. Jean Pritchard later admitted that although the moving gloves were frightening, the way the ghost teased Aunt Maude was funny too.

Maude's gloves reached around the edge of the door like the hands of a huge beast.

MYSTERY MONK

Until now, whatever had been haunting the Pritchards had been invisible. But soon after Maude's visit, Jean and Joe woke up one night to see a hooded figure in the doorway. When they switched on the light, it vanished. Their friends also saw it ~ one of them said it looked like a monk. One visitor even felt it touch her head.

It turned out that there had once been a monastery near the house. Was a monk's ghost on the loose?

The ghost looked like one of the monks who had once lived nearby.

CHASED AWAY

Not long after that, the ghost made a last appearance. Diane and Phillip were watching TV when they suddenly saw the monk through the glass kitchen door. Phillip ran after it, and was just in time to see it disappear into the kitchen floor. That was the last they ever saw or heard of it.

Was the Pontefract poltergeist a hoax? The ghost hunters who investigated the case didn't think so. One of them, Colin Wilson, said that there were so many witnesses and unexplained events that the case only convinced him that ghosts really do exist...

THE BELL WITCH

THIS POLTERGEIST STAYED WITH THE BELL FAMILY OF ROBERTSON COUNTY, TENNESSEE, FOR FOUR WHOLE YEARS. PEOPLE BELIEVED IN WITCHCRAFT AT THAT TIME, SO THE GHOST BECAME KNOWN AS THE BELL WITCH.

Even if they do exist, ghosts and poltergeists hardly ever hurt anyone. The case of the Bell Witch, a poltergeist that plagued the Bell family from 1817 to 1821, is one of the very few hauntings on record in which a victim was apparently murdered by the ghost involved.

NASTY NOISES

As in many poltergeist cases, the haunting began with a series of strange noises. At first the family heard scratching and nibbling noises that sounded like rats gnawing at the furniture. Then they heard the sound of an invisible dog clawing at the wooden floor, and a frantic flapping against the ceiling as if a large, invisible bird were trapped inside a room. But no rats or other animals were found in the house.

SPOOKY SOUNDS

As time went on, the sounds changed. They began to include noisy showers of pebbles clattering on the roof and the slow, scraping sound of a heavy chain being dragged across the floor.

As this old engraving shows, witches were thought to meet with the Devil to receive instructions.

The family got really scared when the unnerving noises began to sound more human. Whatever, or whoever, was haunting the house started to make gurgling and choking noises, and a revolting lip-smacking sound.

At first, the scary noises in their house made the Bells think they had rats.

HAIR HORROR

The ghost gradually became noisier, and eventually it could be felt as well as heard.

One evening, seven-year-old Richard Bell ~ who later wrote an account of the haunting, entitled *Our Family Trouble* ~ was lying in bed when he suddenly felt someone pulling his hair. He couldn't see anyone, but the invisible force pulled so hard that Richard screamed in pain, terrified that his scalp would be ripped off.

At the same time, his sister Betsy, who was 12, screamed as well. The exact same thing was happening to her.

Betsy Bell now became the focus of the haunting. She was slapped on the face by an invisible hand, which left a red mark. She tried spending a night away from the house, but the ghost followed Betsy wherever she was staying and continued to slap her, so she came home. By now, the family feared that they were victims of witchcraft, which many people believed in in those days.

SECRET SPOOK

Betsy's parents, John and Lucy Bell, didn't want to tell anyone about the strange events. John Bell was a prosperous cotton farmer, and his devoutly Christian family was well-respected in the area. The Bells knew that if anyone heard about the supernatural goings-on in their house, they might even be accused of witchcraft themselves.

Anyone, male or female, could be suspected of witchcraft. This picture shows a male and a female witch riding through the air with the Devil.

THE SECRET IS OUT

As things got worse, the family at last decided to confide in a friend, James Johnson, who tried talking to the "witch". As he asked it questions and urged it to speak, its voice gradually changed from a gurgle into a distinctly human whisper.

The witch also became louder and more violent, frequently hitting Betsy and her father, John Bell. Betsy had fainting fits and trouble breathing. Was the spirit taking its energy from her ~ or was she faking it?

A doctor tested this by touching Betsy's throat when the witch was speaking. He said he was sure her larynx was not moving, so the voice could not have been hers.

CAUGHT IN A SHEET

On one occasion, a visitor to the house actually claimed to have caught hold of the spirit. William Porter described how he had been lying in bed when his bedclothes were pulled off him. Porter bravely leaped on them and bundled them up, crying "I have the ghost!" He was sure he had caught something, as the bundle felt heavy and gave off a revolting smell.

For people it liked, the Bell Witch would make oranges, nuts and other foods appear out of thin air.

Porter tried to lug the thing he had caught to the fireplace, planning to throw it into the flames. But the bundle got heavier and heavier, and the stink became so terrible that he was forced to drop the sheets and run from the room. When he went back in, the ghost was gone.

FRIEND OR FOE?

The Bell family's poltergeist was particularly puzzling because it seemed to have two different personalities. It tormented Betsy and her father, but it also had a kinder side. It made nuts appear out of thin air for Lucy Bell when she was ill, calling "Luce, poor Luce, how do you feel now?" Exotic fruit appeared at her Bible meetings, and once the witch produced a basket of bananas, oranges and grapes at a birthday party for one of the children.

MARRIAGE ADVICE

More then three years passed in this way, and the family got used to their strange guest ~ although John Bell was so persecuted by it that he became very depressed.

When Betsy was sixteen, she got engaged to a local boy named Joshua Gardner. She seemed happy and excited about the wedding, but the witch had other ideas. It moaned and groaned, begging "Please, Betsy Bell, don't have Joshua Gardner".

Then it began making disgusting comments about the couple, embarrassing Betsy in front of all her family and friends. At last she was forced to break off the engagement.

DEATHLY DEMISE

The worst, however, was yet to come. John Bell, whom the witch had always hated, became very ill. He took to his bed, but even then the ghost would not leave him alone. It screamed and ranted, threatening to kill him.

Finally, just before Christmas 1820, John Bell slipped into a coma. His son John Junior went to the medicine cabinet, but instead of the prescribed medicine he found an unfamiliar bottle, full of a dark, smoky liquid.

The witch's ghostly voice boasted that it had put the bottle in the cupboard and poisoned John Bell with the contents. "It's useless for you to try and relieve Old Jack," it crowed. "I have got him this time; he will never get up from that bed again!"

The family doctor examined the bottle and decided to test the liquid on the cat. After tasting it, the animal jumped into the air, whirled around, and died. The next day, John Bell was dead too.

"GOODBYE TO ALL!"

The witch now seemed satisfied. After singing some rude songs at John Bell's funeral, it began to fade away. Finally, in the spring of 1821, the family heard something heavy falling down the chimney. A large ball, like a cannonball, rolled out onto the hearth, then burst in a puff of smoke. Then the voice called out: "I'm going, and will be gone for seven years. Goodbye to all!"

THE WITCH IS GONE

The haunting ended that day. Seven years later, there were indeed a few signs of the witch, including scratching sounds and moving bedclothes; but they lasted only two weeks. Before leaving for good, the witch told John Junior that it would return after another 107 years ~ but there is no evidence that it did.

WHAT WAS IT?

Some people thought Betsy Bell had faked the haunting. But there were so many witnesses that this seems unlikely. Ghosthunters who visited the house determined to expose a hoax were defeated by the case.

Perhaps the Bell Witch really was a poltergeist, produced by Betsy's mind. It may have expressed feelings she could not admit to ~ such as hatred of her father, or reluctance to marry Joshua Gardner. However, if it really did murder John Bell, it was the strangest and most powerful poltergeist ever recorded.

Burning was the traditional punishment for those suspected of witchcraft. In this picture, witches are being executed in Germany in 1555.

THE CASE OF ESTHER COX

THIS EXCEPTIONALLY SCARY POLTERGEIST TORMENTED AND TERRIFIED A TEENAGE GIRL IN AMHERST, CANADA IN THE 1870S. IT EVEN THREATENED TO KILL HER - BUT IN THE END, AFTER A SERIES OF APPALLING ATTACKS, ESTHER COX ESCAPED WITH HER LIFE.

Experts think poltergeists may be caused by violent emotions, especially in teenagers, which somehow turn into a terrifying physical force. Could this have been what happened to Esther Cox?

Strange things began to happen to Esther in 1878, when she was 17 ~ just after a traumatic experience. She had been out on a buggy ride with her boyfriend, Bob, when he suddenly drew a gun and told her to follow him into the woods. Esther thought she was going to die. She was only saved when another vehicle approached. Scared of being seen, Bob drove her home, then left town for good.

THE FIRST SIGNS

Just a few days later, Esther and her sister Jane, who lived with their older sister and her husband Daniel Teed, were in their shared bed when they thought they felt something moving. It was as if a mouse or other small animal was trapped inside the mattress.

The moving stopped, and they forgot about it. But the following night it happened again. Trying to investigate, Jane pulled out a box of fabric from under the bed, and the girls were amazed to see it jump into the air. They called their brother-in-law, but he said they must have dreamed it.

STRANGE SICKNESS

The following night, Esther suddenly jumped out of bed and woke Jane, shouting "What's the matter with me? I'm dying!" Lighting a lamp, Jane was astonished to see that Esther's face was as red as a beetroot. Her eyes were bulging and her hair was standing on end. Jane fetched the rest of the family, and they all watched in horror as Esther's body began to swell up like a balloon. Finally, just as they thought it couldn't get any worse, four loud crashes shook the house, and Esther returned to normal.

A DOCTOR CALLS

The family called their doctor, who said Esther was simply suffering from nerves. Then, as he spoke, Esther's pillow began to move. It slid out from under her head and floated in the air next to the bed. Then it slid back. When it started to do the same again, Daniel Teed's brother grabbed hold of it ~ but he couldn't stop it from moving.

Fabric patches and bedclothes were just some of the things that moved by themselves in Esther Cox's house.

MURDEROUS MESSAGE

After that, total pandemonium broke out. Banging and thumping noises began to echo around the room, and the bedclothes jumped off the bed and flew through the air. As the family tried to catch them, they suddenly heard a sharp scraping sound from behind the bed. They turned to look, and saw that some words, in letters almost a foot high, were being scrawled in the plaster on the wall above Esther's head.

They read: "ESTHER COX, YOU ARE MINE TO KILL".

FIRE THREAT

Esther became sick with diptheria, and the haunting died down. But she got better, and the ghost came back ~ this time with a new trick. One night, Esther heard a voice whispering in her ear. It was the ghost, threatening to set the house on fire. Jane called the rest of the family, but no one believed Esther. Despite the strange things they had seen, they reassured her that a ghost couldn't start a fire. At that moment, a lighted match suddenly appeared near the ceiling and fell onto the bed. When Jane put it out, more matches fell around the room.

ON THE MOVE

The family managed to prevent any damage, but when the news got out the villagers of Amherst panicked. All their houses were made of wood, and they knew that if a fire started it would spread quickly. They pressured Daniel Teed to send Esther to live somewhere else.

Esther Cox's house in Amherst, Canada

Esther stayed with various friends ~ but the eerie events just followed her. They even got worse. She got a job at a restaurant, but knives and forks threw themselves at her, sometimes injuring her. Then she worked on a farm. Soon after she arrived, the barn caught fire and burned down.

ACCUSED

Esther was accused of starting the fire, and was tried in court. She was sent to prison, but when friends and villagers explained that she was the victim of a haunting, she was freed. After that, the haunting ended. Some suspected Esther had faked the ghost, but no one could say how ~ and the town of Amherst is still famous for its classic poltergeist case.

ESTHER COX
YOU ARE MINE
TO KILL

GHOSTLY MESSAGES

SOME GHOSTS SEEM TO SEEK OUT SPECIFIC PEOPLE TO BRING THEM A MESSAGE. IN THIS WAY, GHOSTS HAVE REVEALED GUILTY SECRETS, BROUGHT NEWS OF FARAWAY DEATHS, AND EVEN FORETOLD TRAGIC EVENTS.

Many ghosts don't even seem to notice the terrified witnesses who encounter them. But there are some who visit particular people with an urgent purpose in mind.

The most famous ghostly messages come from spirits who warn their victims of impending doom ~ usually their own death or that of someone close to them. No one knows why ghosts seems to be able to predict the future in this way. But once it has happened, there is little the haunted person can do to avoid their fate.

I WILL STAY IN THIS HOUSE

Some poltergeists leave written messages in houses they are haunting.

CRISIS APPARITIONS

A crisis apparition is the name given to the ghost of a person who is dying, or in great danger of some kind. This type of ghost usually appears to a friend, relative or loved one, far away from the scene of the tragedy, as if trying to warn them about what is happening at the time.

Joseph Collier worked on a Mississippi riverboat like this one.

For example, on January 3, 1856, a woman named Mrs. Collier woke up to see her son Joseph standing at the foot of her bed, his head covered in bandages. She knew he should be far away on the riverboat on the Mississippi where he worked. But before she could ask what he was doing, Joseph disappeared.

Two weeks later, news came of Joseph's death. His boat had crashed and a falling mast had hit him on the head. It had happened on January 3 ~ at the very moment when his mother had seen his ghost.

GUILTY GHOSTS

Some ghosts simply have to confess to a murder or other crime they committed during their lives. Only when they have done so, and made amends for their evil ways, can they rest in peace.

For example, a family in Banffshire, Scotland, was haunted for many years by the ghost of a woman in a green dress. One night, the ghost appeared to the family nurse, and began to speak.

The green lady told how, when she had lived in the house, a poor pedlar had come to the door with a roll of beautiful green cloth to sell. But the lady had no time for vagabonds, and ordered her servants to chase the pedlar off her land. As they did so, a fight broke out and the pedlar, outnumbered by the lady's servants, was killed.

The dead pedlar's money and goods were stolen to hide the evidence of his murder.

COVER-UP

The lady was too frightened to tell anyone what had happened. So, instead of confessing to her part in the killing, she had covered up the crime and had the pedlar's body taken away and buried. Then she had taken the pedlar's purse of gold coins and the lovely green cloth he had tried to sell her. She had made it into a dress for herself.

But ever since the pedlar's death, the ghost revealed, she had been burdened with terrible guilt. Even after she herself died, she had been unable to rest. She told the nurse where the stolen money was hidden ~ behind a tapestry in the house ~ and begged her to tell the rest of the family her story.

The nurse told everyone what had happened, and the money was found. The green lady's conscience was cleared and, from then on, she was never seen again.

The green lady's ghost always appeared wearing the dress she had made from the stolen fabric.

THE WOMAN IN WHITE

THIS CLASSIC TALE, IN WHICH A GHOST IN A WHITE GOWN BRINGS NEWS OF AN ARISTOCRAT'S IMMINENT DEATH, COMES FROM 18TH-CENTURY ENGLAND.

Lord Lyttelton, a 35-year-old English noblemen, had an unusual visitor on November 24, 1779. He was lying in his four-poster bed, just after midnight, when he heard what sounded like a bird fluttering nearby. He looked up and saw a strange woman, dressed all in white, standing in his bedchamber.

The woman pointed her finger at Lyttelton accusingly, and then made a chilling prediction: she told him he would be dead within three days. As soon as she had delivered her message, she disappeared.

The ghost that appeared in Lord Lyttelton's bedroom was dressed in white from head to toe.

SOCIETY GOSSIP

Lord Lyttelton was very upset and frightened by what he had seen, and began to worry that he really did only have three days to live. He confided in several of his friends, telling them all about the ghostly woman and her unnerving news. As Lyttelton was a wealthy aristocrat, and was well-known in London, gossip about the ghost soon spread throughout the city.

By the morning of November 27, three days after the ghost had appeared, hundreds of people were waiting to find out whether the spooky prediction would come true. Some even said the Lord was being punished for his self-indulgent lifestyle.

This picture, painted shortly after Lord Lyttelton's spooky experience, shows the ghost appearing to him in his bedroom.

DAY OF RECKONING

Lord Lyttelton went to his country house, Pit Place, to spend what he thought might be the last day of his life. He was despondent, dreading that his death would soon be upon him. But as November 27 wore on, he showed no signs of illness, and by suppertime he began to feel quite relieved. He had invited a group of friends to Pit Place for dinner that evening, and he boldly told his guests that he thought the danger was over.

At 11pm, when he went to bed, Lord Lyttelton was still in good health, and confident that he would survive the night. His servant helped him undress, and was then sent to fetch a teaspoon.

When he returned just a few minutes later, the servant was horrified to find Lord Lyttelton having a violent fit. Just a few moments later, he was dead. The time was just before midnight ~ almost exactly three days after the woman in white's visit.

A TRUE STORY

This ghost story is unusual because so many people knew about the prediction before it came true ~ including the famous author Samuel Johnson, who mentioned the ghost in his writings. This suggests it was not a hoax or a made-up story. Lyttelton could have committed suicide, but that seem unlikely, as he very much wanted to escape the prophecy and stay alive. Maybe he really was visited by a ghost who could foretell the future.

LORD TYRONE'S TERRIBLE TIDINGS

LORD TYRONE HAD PROMISED HIS SISTER HE WOULD COME BACK TO VISIT HER AFTER HIS DEATH. BUT THE NEWS HE BROUGHT WAS TO HAUNT HER FOR THE REST OF HER LIFE.

Lady Beresford and Lord Tyrone lived in 18th-century Ireland, and were as close as a brother and sister could be. Even after they both grew up and got married, they remained best friends. To make sure that even death could not part them, they made a spooky pact. They vowed that whichever of them died first would come back as a ghost to visit the other. But they kept this promise a secret from their partners.

FATEFUL DAY

One morning, years later, Lady Beresford came down to breakfast ashen-faced and trembling. Tied around her wrist was a black velvet ribbon. Her husband, Sir Marcus, asked what was wrong, but Lady Beresford would not tell him. All she would say was that, from that day forward, she would always wear the black ribbon.

Friends and relatives assumed the black velvet ribbon was merely a mark of Lady Beresford's grief.

GRIM NEWS

Then Sir Marcus noticed that his wife seemed anxious for the mail to arrive. He asked her kindly if she was expecting a letter. "I am," she replied. "I expect to hear that Lord Tyrone is dead."

Sir Marcus decided his wife must have had a nightmare. But when the mail did come, Lady Beresford was proved right. A letter brought the news that her dear brother Lord Tyrone had died.

Lady Beresford gradually recovered from her loss, but she never took the black ribbon from her wrist. Everyone assumed she wore it in memory of Lord Tyrone.

BIRTHDAY BLUNDER

Four years later, Sir Marcus Beresford also died, and after a while Lady Beresford married again. She had two daughters and then, on her 48th birthday, she gave birth to a son.

She was still in bed, recovering from having [a baby] when some friends came to visit her. They noticed that she suddenly seemed happier than she had been for years. Then one of the visitors congratulated her on reaching the ripe old age of 47.

She immediately corrected him, saying she was 48, but the friend insisted she was 47. He said he had discussed the matter with Lady Beresford's mother, who had been confused about her age for many years. He had checked the parish register to make sure, and Lady Beresford really was only 47.

NASTY SHOCK

On hearing this, Lady Beresford turned white with fear. "You have signed my death warrant," she said. Then she sent her guests away, saying she needed to rest. She asked just one close friend, Lady Betty Cobb, to stay by her side.

THE TRUTH REVEALED

When the others had gone, Lady Beresford explained to Betty Cobb what had happened all those years ago. She told her about the pact she had made with Lord Tyrone, and how, one night, her brother's ghost had appeared in her bedroom, and told her he was dead.

The ghost also foretold the future. It predicted the death of Sir Marcus four years later, and told Lady Beresford how many children she would have ~ two girls and a boy. It then said that she would die at the age of 47.

Over the years, Lady Beresford had seen nearly all the predictions come true. But when she reached what she believed was her 48th birthday, she thought she had escaped the last and most chilling prophecy. The news that she was really only 47 had destroyed her hopes of survival. She knew she would soon be dead.

WITHERED WRIST

Then Lady Beresford explained why, ever since her eerie encounter, she had always worn the black velvet ribbon around her wrist.

When she had seen her brother's ghost, she had asked it to prove to her that it really was a dead spirit. By way of a reply, the ghostly figure had reached out and touched her on the wrist.

The apparition's finger was as cold as ice, and where it brushed her arm, Lady Beresford saw her skin immediately wither and shrivel into a horrible scar. The ghost warned her never to let another living person see the injury ~ so she had always covered it up with the ribbon.

No one else had ever seen what lay beneath it, and Lady Beresford had vowed that they never would ~ until after she was dead.

No one knows how the touch of a ghost was able to scar Lady Beresford's wrist.

THE END COMES

After she had finished telling her story, Lady Beresford suddenly seemed tired and unwell. She asked Lady Cobb to leave her alone to sleep, and Lady Cobb reluctantly left her bedside. But less than an hour later she suddenly heard the sound of Lady Beresford's bell ringing violently.

She rushed back to the bedroom immediately ~ but she was too late. By the time she got there, Lady Beresford had died.

Approaching the body, Lady Cobb gently pulled the black ribbon from her friend's wrist. Beneath it, she saw that the skin was puckered and scarred ~ just as Lady Beresford had described.

The black velvet ribbon worn by Lady Beresford is thought to have been kept by Lady Cobb, and passed on to her descendants.

THE MOUNTAINEER'S MESSAGE

A LETTER TO A FAMOUS CLIMBER CONTAINED A MESSAGE FROM A MYSTERIOUS GHOST, WARNING OF DISASTER ON AN EXPEDITION TO MOUNT EVEREST. BUT ONLY LATER DID THE FULL TRUTH OF THE GHOST'S PROMISE BECOME CLEAR.

In 1975, the British mountaineer Chris Bonington set off to lead an expedition to Mount Everest. Luckily for Bonington, it was not to be the last of his many mountain adventures ~ but tragedy did lie ahead for one member of his team.

SECRET LETTER

When the expedition left for Nepal, Bonington did not tell the other climbers about a letter he had recently received from a psychic named Clement Williamson. Williamson claimed to have been visited by the ghost of Andrew Irvine, a mountaineer who had died on Everest in 1924.

The ghoul had predicted that Bonington's trip would end in disaster. But Williamson had not given the full details of the message. Instead he had written them down, sealed them and locked them in a vault in the Bank of England, in London.

PHANTOM FIGURE

The expedition went ahead, and the team made good progress. On the night of September 26, a climber named Nick Estcourt was making his way from Camp 4 to Camp 5, high up on the snowy slopes. As he trudged on, Estcourt suddenly had a strange feeling that he was being followed. He looked back, and saw the figure of another climber, toiling up the mountainside below him. Then, suddenly, the figure vanished. Estcourt radioed Camp 4 to ask if anyone was following him ~ but no one was.

TRAGEDY STRIKES

The following afternoon, another member of the team, a film cameraman named Mick Burke, was near to reaching the summit. He was so close that he pressed on, despite high winds and a blinding blizzard blowing around the peak. He was never seen alive again.

BACK HOME

Back in London, Bonington went to the Bank of England and opened the sealed letter. It said that during the expedition, a ghost would appear on Everest ~ and that one of the climbers would die.

CATCHING A KILLER

*IF GHOSTS REALLY EXIST, THE MOST
USEFUL THING THEY COULD DO
WOULD BE TO COME BACK AND
REVEAL SECRET INFORMATION
THAT ONLY THEY COULD KNOW.
THAT'S WHAT THE GHOST OF
TERESITA BASA DID IN 1977 - AND
THE EVIDENCE IT GAVE HELPED TO
CATCH HER MURDERER.*

The curious case of Teresita Basa baffled investigators. The 48-year-old Chicago nurse had been murdered ~ viciously stabbed to death in her apartment ~ and all her jewels appeared to be missing. But there were no signs that the apartment had been broken into. The killer could only have been someone Teresita knew ~ but who?

TERESITA RETURNS

The police were at a loss, and it looked as though the case would never be solved. Then, a few weeks after Teresita's death, her friend Remy Chua had a spooky experience.

Remy was also a nurse, one of Teresita's colleagues at the hospital. She was sitting in the rest room at work, having a break, when suddenly she had a strong feeling that there was someone else in the room. She turned to look ~ and, floating in the air right next to her, she saw Teresita's face.

Remy ran screaming from the room and told her fellow workers what she had seen. They all went to check the rest room, but the ghost had gone. However, that was not to be the end of the haunting.

FACE FRIGHT

From that day on, Teresita's ghost began to visit Remy regularly. She often saw it at work ~ sometimes just a face, and sometimes a whole body ~ and she also had several dreams in which her dead friend appeared to her.

Over time, the ghostly apparitions started to change. Remy noticed that, in her dreams and visions, another figure had begun to appear alongside Teresita ~ the figure of a man. His face gradually became clearer, and one day Remy realized that she recognized him. His name was Allan Showery, and he also worked at the hospital, as a porter.

Remy didn't know what to do. There was no evidence linking Showery to the murder, and she certainly didn't want to make false accusations.

Did Showery really go to fix Teresita's TV ~ or did he have a more evil plan?

VOICE OF TRUTH

As if to make sure of her message, Teresita's ghost now tried a new approach ~ it began to speak. Remy started to slip into strange trances, during which Teresita's voice would come out of her mouth.

The voice accused Showery, saying: "Tell them that Al came to fix my television, and then he killed me". It added that the murderer had given the stolen jewels to his girlfriend. The voice went on to name a list of people who would be able to identify Teresita's jewels, and even provided a telephone number for one of them.

WAS IT HIM?

When Remy Chua's husband told the police what had been going on, they had their doubts. Eventually, though, they agreed to interview Allan Showery, and found that at least part of the message was correct: he admitted he had agreed to fix Teresita's TV. But, he said, he had not actually been to her apartment.

Next the police tried Allan Showery's girlfriend, and at her apartment they found a ring Showery had given her. Then they called the number Teresita's ghost had given. It turned out to be one of her cousins, who confirmed that the ring was Teresita's.

COURT CASE

Showery was arrested and charged with murder, but his lawyers argued that a ghost could not be a reliable witness. In the end, the judge ordered a retrial.

Then, just before the second trial began, Showery gave in. He confessed to the murder, and was sent to prison. If it hadn't been for the ghost, he would never even have been a suspect.

The discovery of some of Teresita Basa's stolen jewels led to Allan Showery's arrest.

GHOST HUNTING

SOME PEOPLE ARE SO INTERESTED IN GHOSTS, THEY SPEND THEIR LIVES VISITING HAUNTED HOUSES, TRYING TO SEE SPOOKS AND PHANTOMS. SOME GHOST HUNTERS ALSO TRY TO SPOT HOAX HAUNTINGS AND HELP RESTLESS SPIRITS FIND PEACE.

The more a ghost hunter can measure and record about a haunted place, the easier it is to figure out what's going on. For example, ghosts are often associated with a chill in the air ~ so ghost hunters check to see if a temperature change coincides with a ghostly appearance.

ANIMAL DETECTIVES

Ghost hunters sometimes take animals to the site of a reported haunting, to see if they react to an invisible presence. It often seems that animals may be able to see ghosts when we can't. In one case in Kentucky, U.S.A., a ghost hunter took a rat, a cat, a dog and a rattlesnake into a haunted house.

RESPONSE

All the animals except the rat reacted badly to a particular chair in one of the rooms. The cat snarled at the chair, the rattlesnake reared up to strike it, and the dog ran away from it. But when taken into another room, the animals all relaxed.

However, this doesn't mean that animals really do see ghosts. It could just be that they are sensitive to something else. For example, dogs are much more sensitive to noise than humans are, and can detect sounds we can't hear. Maybe animals can also sense a magnetic field, or some other type of invisible energy such as radio waves.

Rattlesnakes seem to be able to sense something strange in a "haunted" environment.

EQUIPMENT

Here are some of the tools ghost hunters can use:

• Camera or camcorder to photograph ghosts.

• Log book for recording strange events and noting who is there when they happen, and squared paper for drawing maps.

• Tape measure for checking to see if objects have moved.

• Some ghost hunters use an Environmental Monitoring Unit or EMU, which measures temperature, vibrations, air movements and so on.

• An audio tape recorder can sometimes capture spooky sounds no one noticed at the time.

• Powder or sugar for detecting fingerprints and footprints.

• Many modern ghost hunters use a computer to record and analyze their results.

GOODBYE GHOSTS

Some ghost hunters claim they can try to stop hauntings by finding the bones of the restless spirit's body and burying them, in an attempt to lay the ghost to rest.

Borley Rectory, the haunted house that was investigated by Harry Price.

This happened at Borley Rectory (see page 15) in 1943, when ghost hunter Harry Price found some bones which he thought belonged to a ghostly nun who had been seen in the rectory garden. He had the bones buried, but unfortunately this failed to work: the nun was seen again in the years that followed.

SPOOK SCIENCE

A scientific approach can sometimes explain ghosts away, as Vic Tandy's story shows. One night, Vic was alone in the lab where he worked. He suddenly saw a shape out of the corner of his eye, and turned to look, but there was no one there. The ghostly vision made him feel very uncomfortable. His colleagues had also seen strange things in the lab, and some of them thought it was haunted.

SOUND POWER

The next day, Vic brought his fencing blade to work to repair it. When he put it in a clamp, it began to vibrate. Puzzled, Vic moved it around the room. He found that the effect was strongest in the middle of the lab, and guessed that it was caused by infrasound, a low-frequency sound too deep for humans to hear. Tests proved that a low sound wave was coming from a fan in the room. Infrasound can make people feel shivery ~ which explained why Vic's colleagues had felt uneasy. It can also vibrate the eyeball, which could explain why Vic thought he saw a blurry shape.

GHOST HUNTERS

As these cases show, the attitude ghost hunters have to their work may have an effect on their findings. Investigators who believe in ghosts tend to report genuine ghosts, while a scientist like Vic Tandy is more likely to look for another explanation.

Some ghost hunters may even be fakes themselves. The most famous ghost hunter of all, Harry Price, was accused of hoaxing the Borley Rectory haunting in order to make a name for himself.

Vic Tandy's laboratory seemed haunted ~ but wasn't.

GHOSTS OF THE SEA

ACCORDING TO SAILORS' STORIES, THE OCEANS ARE PLAGUED BY HAUNTINGS - STRANGE DISAPPEARANCES, RESTLESS SPIRITS, AND EVEN ENTIRE GHOST SHIPS.

For hundreds of years, sailors have told tales of monsters, ghosts and other strange sights they've seen at sea. Most of these stories are probably completely made up ~ but there are so many of them, perhaps a few are true...

GOING MISSING

The sea is a dangerous place, and it's not unusual for a boat to disappear in a storm, or for a sailor to be swept away. But some seafarers seem to have been carried off by more mysterious forces ~ such as the crew of the *Mary Celeste*. This famous ship was found drifting in December 1872, a month after leaving New York on a voyage to Italy. It had been abandoned ~ but there were no signs of a struggle, a storm or a pirate attack.

On the captain's breakfast table was a boiled egg, opened but uneaten. Nearby, a music book lay open on his wife's musical keyboard. But the captain and his wife, their daughter, and the eight-man crew were never seen again.

RESTLESS SOULS

Boats are often haunted by dead crew members ~ such as the German submarine officer who kept appearing after his death in an explosion (see page 56). Seafarers also report seeing phantom ships ~ the ghosts of sunken vessels. They usually appear surrounded by a red or yellow glow, and are said to bring bad luck to anyone who has the misfortune to see them.

In the past, many sailors feared being attacked by a sea serpent ~ a huge, snake-like creature which was said to wrap itself around a ship, causing it to sink.

DANGEROUS LIFE

Why should so many ghosts have been reported at sea? There are several possible explanations. Some people believe that ghosts are the spirits of people who died in violent circumstances. Many people have died violently at sea ~ in storms, shipwrecks, and naval battles. They were usually "buried" by being thrown overboard. Perhaps their souls, far from home, cannot rest in their watery graves and come back as unhappy ghosts.

Another explanation is that the loneliness and harshness of life at sea can sometimes drive sailors insane. They can suffer hallucinations ~ seeing things that aren't there.

For example, in the days of sailing ships, sailors who were becalmed (stuck in one place with no wind) sometimes suffered from a terrible disease called calenture. They went insane and imagined the waves were green fields. Some sailors drowned trying to run across them. Perhaps similar hallucinations at sea can make people think they've seen ghosts, demons or phantom ships.

This famous ghost ship, the *Libera Nos*, is said to sail the world with a crew of skeletons, bringing tragedy to any ship in its path. It is supposed to be the ghost of a haunted ship which sank in a storm in 1871.

SHIPS IN THE SKY

One of the strangest sights at sea is a mirage, an image of something that is really too far away to see. Mirages happen when layers of warm and cold air cause light to bend. Sometimes a reflection of a faraway ship appears, floating in the sky. Mirages could explain some of the "ghost" ships that sailors have seen.

However, there are still several spooky sea stories that have never been properly explained. On the following pages, you can read about some of the scariest.

THE *FLYING DUTCHMAN*

THE FLYING DUTCHMAN IS THE MOST FAMOUS OF ALL GHOST SHIPS. IT IS SAID TO BRING A CURSE ON ANYONE WHO SEES IT, AND HAS TERRIFIED SAILORS FOR OVER A CENTURY.

The story of the *Flying Dutchman* is a sea legend. It exists in several versions, and has even been made into an opera. Yet behind the romantic tales may lie a genuine haunting.

CRAZY CAPTAIN

No one knows for sure where the *Flying Dutchman* story came from, but most versions of the legend begin with the story of a nineteenth-century Dutch merchant ship. The vessel was rounding the Cape of Good Hope, at the southern tip of South Africa, on its way from Europe to the East Indies (the old name for southeast Asia).

In some sailor's tales, the stricken ghost ship appears swathed in a spooky glow.

STORM

As it changed direction, the ship ran into a violent storm ~ but the captain, proud of his reputation for making fast journeys, would not put into port. The crew begged him to at least lower the sails, but he refused, unwilling to allow even a few hours' delay.

MARINE MURDER

The storm grew worse, and when parts of the rigging began to crash onto the deck, one of the crewmen decided to take action. He tried to wrestle the ship's wheel away from the captain in order to steer the ship to safety. But the furious captain grabbed the man and hurled him overboard into the waves, never to be seen again.

Legend has it that an angel then appeared and condemned the cruel captain to a terrible punishment. After his death, he was destined to roam the seas forever, on board a ghostly vessel, bringing terror and tragedy to any ship that came near him.

Route of Merchant ship ......

Storm hit here ~

Cape of Good Hope

SINKING

The captain's ship was swallowed by the waves, and he drowned. Ever since, so the story goes, the phantom ship, known as the *Flying Dutchman*, has sailed the world, enveloped in an eerie mist.

SIGHTINGS AT SEA

The story sounds like a fairy tale ~ but sailors have often reported seeing ghost ships, and many of them believed they had encountered the *Flying Dutchman*. One of the most famous reports came from Prince George of England, who later became King George V.

In 1881, when he was 16, he was a naval cadet on a British frigate, the *H.M.S. Inconstant*, off the coast of Australia. His journal entry for July 11 began: "At 4:00 a.m. the *Flying Dutchman* crossed our bows." The journal describes "a strange red light, as of a phantom ship all aglow, in the midst of which light the mast, spars and sails of a brig two hundred yards distant stood out in strong relief." In total, eleven men on the *Inconstant* saw the ghostly vessel, and two more ships in the same convoy also spotted it.

TRAGIC FALL

Whether or not the ship the Prince saw was the *Flying Dutchman*, as he believed, it certainly seemed to bring the traditional bad luck with it. At 10:45 the same morning, the seaman who had been the first to see the strange ship fell from the top of one of the Inconstant's tall masts. He was killed instantly as he smashed onto the deck.

WARTIME WITNESS

Another famous witness was Admiral Karl Dönitz, a German commander in the Second World War. He was sure a ship he and his crew saw in the Indian Ocean was the *Flying Dutchman*. Even though they only glimpsed it for a short while, Dönitz reported that the entire crew was terrified by the experience ~ in fact, his men were even more afraid of the ghost ship than they were of their war enemies.

THE HAUNTED SUBMARINE

IN THE FIRST WORLD WAR, SUBMARINES KNOWN AS U-BOATS WERE AMONG THE GERMANS' MOST SUCCESSFUL WEAPONS. BUT ONE OF THE SUBS SEEMED TO BE AFFLICTED BY A POWERFUL CURSE...

U-boats are the most famous submarines ever built. They patrolled the seas during the First World War, hiding beneath the waves and blasting enemy ships with torpedoes. But one U-boat, UB65, scared not only its enemies, but also its own crew.

BAD START

UB65 was built in 1916, in the middle of the war. Even before it was completed, the vessel became associated with bad luck. Two men were killed when a steel girder fell on them during construction, and three more died when fumes overcame them as they were fitting the engine. And on the submarine's first trial run, a seaman was swept into the sea and drowned.

GHOST ON DECK

Then, as the torpedoes were being loaded for the submarine's first mission, one of them accidentally exploded, killing five more men. One of them was Lieutenant Richter, the ship's vice-captain.

Before the submarine set sail, a terrified crew member came running to the captain. He said he had seen the ghost of Lieutenant Richter walking up the gangplank onto the deck, where it had stood with its arms folded, staring at him.

The captain went to the deck himself. The ghost had gone, but another sailor named Petersen was there. He too had seen the ghost, and was sitting on the deck, frozen in terror. He was so frightened that he jumped ship, refusing to sail on the UB65.

The machinery inside the U-boats made them so hot, cramped and unpleasant that crew members sometimes went insane.

OUT TO SEA

When UB65 finally set off on its first cruise, things went well. The sub's torpedoes sank two enemy ships and damaged two more. For three weeks, there was no sign of the ghost. But one day, as the boat was patrolling the English Channel in a storm, the lookout was amazed to see a man standing on the deck among the waves, his arms folded. The hatches had all been closed to prevent the U-boat from being swamped. How could anyone have climbed outside?

Then, as the figure turned around, the lookout realized it was Lieutenant Richter ~ the vice-captain who had been dead for a month.

This picture of U-boats at sea shows the type of deck where Lieutenant Richter's ghost was seen.

CRACKDOWN

Gossip about the ghost spread, and when UB65 returned to port, crew members began to ask to be transferred to other vessels. To put a stop to the stories, the fleet commander, Admiral Schroeder, came to examine the ship. He spent a night on board, declaring the ghost stories were nonsense. When the sub set sail again, the captain ordered that anyone who reported seeing ghosts would be punished.

For a while, the new regime worked. No one mentioned the ghost, and work continued as normal. As the war went on, however, the Germans began to suffer heavy losses, and the U-boat crewmen knew they had little chance of returning home alive. Living in overheated, cramped conditions, they began to call the U-boats "steel coffins".

DISASTER

Finally, the pressure got too much for one of the gunners on UB65. He ran screaming into the control room, yelling that he had seen the ghost, and had to be given drugs to calm him down. As soon as he was allowed to leave his bunk, he threw himself overboard and drowned.

After that, things went from bad to worse. An officer was swept away by a wave, the engineer fell and broke his leg, and another man died during an attack from enemy ships. Morale was low when the boat returned to port; but there was no time to waste. UB65 was needed in action. So, in July 1918, the sub set out on another mission, which was to be its last.

THE END COMES

The final sighting of the UB65 was reported by Lieutenant Forster, the captain of an American submarine. On July 10, he was cruising in the Atlantic, off the south coast of Ireland, when he came across a German submarine, listing badly and apparently abandoned. It was UB65.

As Forster warily edged his ship closer, the enemy sub was suddenly ripped apart in a massive explosion. It quickly sank ~ but as it did so, Forster thought he *could* see someone on board after all. A figure in uniform seemed to be standing on the deck, with his arms folded, staring at the conning tower. Had Lieutenant Richter stayed with his doomed vessel until the end?

Lieutenant Richter's ghost always appeared on the deck of UB65, staring at the conning tower, which the crew used as a lookout post.

THE EILEAN MÓR MYSTERY

FOR CENTURIES, PEOPLE HAVE GONE MISSING IN MYSTERIOUS CIRCUMSTANCES AND NEVER RETURNED - ESPECIALLY AT SEA. THE CURIOUS CASE OF THE EILEAN MÓR LIGHTHOUSE IS A CLASSIC EXAMPLE.

Eilean Mór means "big island" in Gaelic ~ but in fact Eilean Mór is just a tiny island off the coast of Scotland. There are no towns or villages there, only a lonely lighthouse. It was here, in the stormy December of 1900, that one of the most famous disappearances of all time took place.

LONELY LIFE

In those days, lighthouse-keepers lived isolated lives, far away from friends and family. They had no telephone, so when they were on duty they had only each other for company.

In the dark, harsh Scottish winter, it was important that lighthouses kept working, so the four lighthouse-keepers at Eilean Mór could not all go home for Christmas. Only one of them, Joseph Moore, had shore leave that month, from December 6 to 26. When he left, the lighthouse was running smoothly and his colleagues, James Ducat, Donald McArthur and Thomas Marshall, were all in good health. But he was never to see any of them again.

GONE MISSING

When Joseph Moore returned to the island after Christmas, the Eilean Mór lighthouse was deserted and its light had gone out. Nothing seemed to be missing, except for two sets of boots and oilskins, which were waterproof clothes, belonging to the lighthouse-keepers. Puzzled, Moore searched everywhere, but he could find no evidence of any struggle, no note ~ no sign of his friends at all.

Had one of them fallen into the raging sea, and the other two lost their lives trying to help him? This seemed unlikely, as all three were experienced seamen who would not have taken such a risk.

Had they tried to leave the island and go home? That was impossible, as their boat had not been taken. And no bodies were ever recovered.

After the Eilean Mór disappearances, sailors said they had seen a ghostly boat heading for the island.

LOG CLUES

Moore checked the log book where the keepers kept a record of the weather and their daily routines. It showed that a huge storm had battered Eilean Mór on December 12 ~ Thomas Marshall had written: "Never have I seen such a storm". But it was not the storm that had carried the keepers away. The entry for December 15 read: "1 p.m. Storm ended. Sea calm. God is over all." After that, the entries stopped.

TALL TALES

So what had happened to the lighthouse-keepers of Eilean Mór? When the story got out, local people said they thought the island was haunted, and that the three men had joined the many ghosts who lived there. Two sailors who had passed through the area on December 15 on board their ship, the *Fairwind*, claimed they had seen a boat full of ghosts and demons, heading for the Eilean Mór lighthouse.

Later, a poem about Eilean Mór romanticized the story, suggesting that the keepers had been magically changed into huge black ravens.

But none of these tales helps to unravel what really did happen to the three men. Like the crew of the *Mary Celeste* (see page 52), they seem simply to have vanished, in calm weather, with no explanation at all.

Could aliens be responsible for mysterious disappearances?

MISSING PEOPLE

Many people go missing suddenly and mysteriously, just as the Eilean Mór lighthouse-keepers did. Some turn up again, but many never do. Of course, some disappearances can be explained: the missing person may have run away from home, or had a tragic accident. But other unexplained disappearances have led to some scarier suggestions.

For example, some people believe that aliens regularly kidnap humans and take them away to study. Others claim that it's possible to "slip" into another dimension, a different time period or even a parallel universe, through some kind of hole in the universe which science has not yet understood. But it is impossible to test these theories ~ so strange stories such the case of Eilean Mór remain a mystery.

Some said the men had been turned into ravens ~ large, black birds which often appear in ghost stories.

GHOSTLY PHOTOS

THERE ARE HUNDREDS OF PHOTOGRAPHS WHICH APPEAR TO SHOW GHOSTS - BUT GHOSTLY PHOTOS ARE VERY EASY TO FAKE. ONLY A FEW ARE STILL UNEXPLAINED. DO THESE PICTURES REALLY REVEAL PHANTOMS ON FILM?

Even if ghosts do exist, they are notoriously hard to pin down. Most appear only for a few seconds, vanishing when witnesses try to get closer.

However, there is no shortage of "ghost" photos. A quick search on the Internet will reveal dozens of them. Sadly, most of these are hoaxes or double exposures. When a camera doesn't wind properly, it's common for a picture of a person to be superimposed on another photo. This can end up looking like a transparent, ghostly figure.

The image on the right is one of the few genuinely unexplained ghost photos. It was taken by Reverend Lord in his church in Newby, England (see opposite page).

In this photo of a banquet, a tall, hooded figure stands at the top of the table. No one who was at the banquet could remember seeing him there...

SPOOKY SNAPS

There are only a few ghost photos that have never been proved to be fakes. Oddly, some of the most convincing ones were taken when the photographer couldn't even see a ghost. The spooks only became visible when the film was developed.

This happened to a priest, the Reverend K. F. Lord, who took a picture of the altar of his church in Newby, England in the early 1960s (see opposite page). Lord didn't see anything strange when he was in the church ~ but when the picture was developed, it showed a tall, hooded, very scary figure, standing on the altar steps.

Another photographer, Derek Stafford, visited a graveyard one night in 1990 in order to take photos of the floodlit gravestones. He was later shocked to find that he had also taken a photo of a dark, hooded monk-like figure looming over the graves.

When local people saw the photo, however, they weren't surprised. They said it was a well-known local ghost, the Black Abbot, who had often been seen walking through that graveyard.

MISTY SHAPES

Many ghosts seem to show up in photographs as vague, misty white areas. Marks like this could be caused by reflections, or by light leaking into the camera. But in some cases they may show real ghosts. One example involves a toddler named Greg Maxwell.

One day in 1991, when Greg was two, he suddenly pointed upwards as his photograph was being taken, and said "Old Nana's here". He meant his great-grandmother, who had recently died. When the photo was developed, it showed Greg looking at a misty white shape. Was this his Nana's ghost?

No one except Greg saw anything odd when this photo was taken, but a white shape appeared in the photo.

SPOOKY HAPPENINGS

WHAT MAKES SOMETHING SPOOKY, INSTEAD OF JUST UNUSUAL? THINGS THAT CAN'T BE EXPLAINED ARE OFTEN KNOWN AS THE PARANORMAL ~ STRANGE, UNCANNY OR WEIRD EVENTS THAT CAN SEND A SHIVER DOWN YOUR SPINE...

The "paranormal" includes all sorts of mysterious phenomena: sightings of aliens; strange creatures such as the abominable snowman and the Loch Ness monster; curses and jinxes; people going missing; and people who seem to be able to levitate, see into the future, or read other people's minds.

The abominable snowman is a huge, half-human beast said to roam mountainous areas.

Not all types of paranormal phenomena are bad. Some, such as telepathy ~ which means communicating using your mind ~ could be very useful if we ever learn to understand and control them.

Yet people often find paranormal events scary, because they are unexplained and mysterious. The stories told in this section of the book include a Celtic curse, a lonely haunted road, and a house in Spain where strange faces appear in the floor.

MAGIC AND SCIENCE

Paranormal events are outside our current scientific knowledge, but that doesn't mean we'll never understand them. For example, levitation, or floating into the air, is currently a "paranormal" event. According to the laws of physics, it's not normal for things or people to float around on thin air. Yet witnesses claim they have seen it happen. This could mean that levitation has a scientific explanation which we have not yet discovered.

People have been reported to levitate, or float into the air, during poltergeist hauntings.

Do aliens from other worlds visit our planet? Some people say they have seen them and their spacecraft.

Many scientific phenomena must have seemed like magic before they were properly understood. For example, magnetism makes things seem to move by themselves, and solar eclipses make the sun go dark during the day ~ but these things are no longer seen as strange. Perhaps paranormal events will one day be explained in the same way.

HOAXES AND FAKES

The other explantion for many spooky happenings is that they are faked. Because they are so unusual, paranormal events are very interesting. Everyone wants to hear about them and be amazed. And that means people can gain fame and fortune by faking ghosts, UFOs, and all kinds of magical abilities. For example, the Lutz family made a lot of money from the story of their haunted house at Amityville (see page 10). Eventually, investigators began to suspect that the story was a hoax.

There are also hundreds of faked photos of aliens and monsters. And, for hundreds of years, people have been pretending to see into the future, heal wounds by magic, or read minds. All these fakes make it extra hard for investigators to find and study genuine strange phenomena.

TESTING TIMES

Apart from hoaxers, there are other problems for scientists who want to study weird wonders and strange sightings. Paranormal events ~ such as a cold chill in a haunted house, the appearance of the Loch Ness monster, or a poltergeist throwing something across a room ~ are rare and unpredictable. They are usually reported by very few witnesses, who may have been so excited or frightened by what they have seen that they were not able to observe events with a clear head. So it's very hard for scientists to be sure what happened.

This famous photo of the Loch Ness Monster seems to prove that a dinosaur-like creature lives in the Loch. But many people think the photo is a fake.

SPOOK RESEARCH

However, despite all these problems, there are several organizations devoted to studying and explaining the paranormal. One of the most famous is the Society for Psychical Research (SPR). It was started in 1882 in London, England, at the height of a craze for Spiritualism (trying to contact the dead) and telepathy. There is now also an American SPR, based in New York. Researchers from these organizations try to study reports of paranormal events with an open mind. They keep detailed records of all the hauntings and strange sightings they investigate.

In this telepathy experiment, a subject tries to send and receive messages using only her mind.

THE HAIRY HANDS

IN THIS HORRIBLE HAUNTING, WHICH PLAGUES A LONELY MOORLAND ROAD, THERE IS NO GHOST - ONLY A HIDEOUS PAIR OF HANDS WHICH HATE ALL FORMS OF TRANSPORTATION.

Dartmoor, a high, windy wilderness in the south west of England, is famous for its spinechilling local legends and spooky atmosphere. There are many tales about ghosts, demons and strange creatures that are said to roam its lonely landscape. But it is the strangest story of all ~ the tale of two hairy hands ~ that seems the most convincing.

Lonely roads can be scary ~ but is the road to Two Bridges really haunted?

CREEPY CRASH

The most famous account of the hands comes from 1926, when a doctor took two children for a ride across the moor in his motorcycle side-car. They were the children of his friend, a deputy governor at nearby Dartmoor Prison, where the doctor worked.

As they sped along the road from Postbridge to Two Bridges, the motorcycle suddenly veered dangerously. The doctor shouted to the children to jump clear, and they did so just in time to escape alive as the vehicle crashed into the roadside. The doctor was killed at once.

HANDS

When they were rescued, the children claimed they had seen a pair of huge, hairy hands on the motorcycle handlebars. The police thought they must have seen the doctor's driving gloves and mistaken them for hands. But just two months later, there was another crash. An army officer was riding his motorcycle along the same road when he felt something touch his hands. To his horror, he saw two large, hairy hands closing over his own. Suddenly they wrenched the handlebars aside, driving him off the road.

The hairy hands seem to have a particular hatred of motorcycles.

ANCIENT TALES

The motorcycle riders weren't the only ones who had experienced the hairy hands. It turned out that they had been seen on previous occasions ~ years before motor vehicles were invented. Tales of phantom fists, which grabbed the reins from riders, had often been told in earlier centuries.

These stories were gathered together in a book called *Supernatural England*, by a writer named Eric Maple. All the tales came from the same part of Dartmoor ~ the lonely road between Postbridge and Two Bridges.

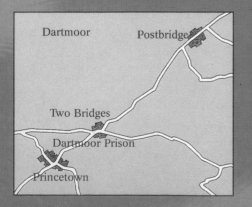

The haunted road crosses an empty stretch of Dartmoor, in England

MORE ENCOUNTERS

In 1989, a prison officer had a fright when the hands tried to steer his car off the same road. He couldn't see them, but he felt them grabbing the steering wheel, and only just managed to control the car. Another witness, Florence Warwick, parked by the road to look at her car manual. She was shocked to see two disembodied, hairy hands clawing at the car window. They vanished, and Florence escaped without an accident.

Several drivers have died on the same route. In 1960 a car was found overturned at the roadside, its driver crushed to death ~ but there was nothing wrong with the vehicle. Was this motorist another victim of the evil hands?

All the witness who have seen the hands have described them in the same way ~ as large, muscular and very hairy.

WHAT ARE THEY?

The deadly activities of the hairy hands make them very unusual. Most ghosts and other paranormal entities, if they exist, are completely harmless; but the hands seem to have been responsible for at least one violent death.

No one has been able to explain this bizarre haunting. Experts have found the remains of an ancient bronze age village nearby. Do the hands belong to the ghost of an early human settler? Even if they do, their attacks on innocent drivers and riders remain a chilling mystery.

THE GHOSTLY FACES OF BÉLMEZ

ARE THE PEREIRAS FAKING THE STRANGE FACES THAT APPEAR IN THEIR KITCHEN FLOOR? IN OVER TWO DECADES OF THIS VERY ODD HAUNTING, NO ONE HAS BEEN ABLE TO EXPLAIN EXACTLY WHAT IS HAPPENING.

One morning in August 1971, Maria Gomez Pereira came downstairs, just as she did every morning, to the kitchen of her house in Bélmez, in the Spanish province of Andalusia.

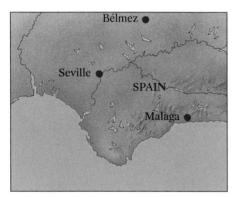

The village of Bélmez was little-known until the spooky faces put it on the map.

She had lived in the house for years, having moved there when she married a local farmer. But today something was different. On the concrete kitchen floor was a strange mark. It reminded Maria of a face.

CHANGING FACE

At first, Maria thought the image must be a stain. She tried to scrub it off, but it wouldn't disappear. Then, as the days went by, something strange began to happen. The face changed.

STARING

It gradually became clearer and more detailed until, after a week, the Pereira family could see all its features as it stared spookily up at them.

Gossip spread around the village, and people soon began coming to see the face for themselves. To put a stop to the disturbance, Maria's son Miguel took a hammer and smashed the part of the floor where the face was. Then he cemented it over.

BACK AGAIN

Miguel's measures didn't last long. A week later, a new face started to form ~ this time of an old man. First the eyes appeared, then the nose, lips and chin came into view.

Once more, villagers began flocking to the house, and the police were called to control the crowds. Eventually the local council sent a workman to cut out the face and take it away for tests.

This photo shows one of the Bélmez faces.

After it had been dug up, the face stopped changing. But the experts who examined it couldn't find out how it had been made. The concrete seemed perfectly normal. So the face was returned to the Pereiras.

MORE FACES

After another week of peace, a new face began to take shape on the floor. Miguel destroyed it immediately, but as soon as he had done so, yet another one appeared. Eventually, he gave up ~ and the floor gradually became covered in an array of eerie images.

One showed a young woman, with her hair flying as if blown by a breeze. Other, smaller faces appeared around her. Another face seemed to belong to a child, and one, of a bald old man, became known as "the bald one".

Smashing the floor with a hammer failed to put a stop to the appearance of the strange faces.

Even stranger, the faces continued to change, even after they were fully developed. One of the images, of a beautiful woman, grew until it included her hand, which was holding a flower. Over time, the shape of the flower changed until it became a cup.

Some faces lasted for several months, while others came and went within a day ~ sometimes even forming as people watched. Several photographs were taken of them, but no one has ever been caught painting the images onto the floor.

PUZZLED PROFESSOR

Not surprisingly, the faces attracted the attention of investigators. One, named Professor de Argumosa, conducted a strict experiment to see if the faces were being faked. He took photographs of the floor, then covered it with foil which he sealed at the edges. When the foil was removed, the faces had changed ~ even though no one had been able to touch them.

The professor also made several tape recordings in the Pereiras' kitchen. The room seemed silent at the time, but when the tapes were played back, dreadful sounds of screaming and groaning could be heard, along with murmuring voices.

The faces grew and changed even when Professor de Argumosa had sealed them under a foil covering.

GHOSTS?

Argumosa decided to research the history of the village. He found that in the 17th century a whole family had been brutally put to death in the Bélmez area. Locals also recalled that the street was said to have been built over an old cemetery. And indeed, when part of the floor was dug up, human bones were unearthed ~ including two headless skeletons. Were these the victims of the murder, trying to make their presence felt by producing the frightening faces?

When investigators dug up the floor of the Péreira's kitchen, they found human bones ~ including two skeletons whose heads had been chopped off.

MYSTERY

The bodies found under the floor were never identified, but the faces kept appearing, and continue to do so to this day, making the house in Bélmez a tourist attraction. Scientists believe there must be a simple explanation ~ but no one has ever been caught faking the images, and several witnesses have seen them forming right in front of their eyes. So, if the faces are being hoaxed, no one has ever found out how.

CURSE OF THE HEXHAM HEADS

CAN OBJECTS REALLY BE CURSED? TWO SMALL CARVED HEADS, FOUND IN 1972, CERTAINLY SEEMED TO HAVE A STRANGE, EVIL POWER. EVERYONE WHO LOOKED AFTER THEM - INCLUDING TWO SENSIBLE SCIENTISTS - ENDED UP BEING HORRIBLY HAUNTED.

The strange story of the mysterious cursed heads begins in 1972, when 11-year-old Colin Robson and his little brother Leslie were clearing weeds in the garden of their house in Hexham, in the north of England. While they were digging, they came across a curious round object, half-buried in the ground.

Cleaning off the dirt, they saw that what they had found was a small, roughly head-shaped carving, about 5cm (2in) wide. Leslie soon found a second, similar head buried nearby.

This photo shows two accurate replicas of the mysterious Hexham heads, which have themselves now been lost.

The "girl" head had pointed features, and many people who saw it thought it was the scarier of the two heads.

The "boy" head had a broader, flatter face and smaller eyes.

HEADS IN THE HOUSE

The boys took the two strange sculptures indoors to show their parents. After washing the heads, they saw that they were slightly different. One, which they named the "girl" head because it looked like a witch, had a narrow, pointed face, a pointed nose, and large hollows for eyes. It seemed to be shaped out of a rough material.

The other head, which the family named the "boy" head, had a broader face, with a straight nose and small eyes. It looked and felt as though it was carved out of a pale, grainy stone.

EERIE EFFECTS

At first, the Robsons were just curious, not frightened. But as soon as the heads came into the house, strange things began to happen. A mirror frame was found in a frying pan, smashed to pieces. A shower of broken glass fell onto a bed. The heads began to spin around by themselves, and the boys said they saw an eerie light glowing in the garden at the spot where they had been found.

BEDROOM BEAST

However, the scariest event of all took place next door, where the Dodd family lived. Ellen Dodd was looking after her 10-year-old son Brian, who was ill in bed. She had turned out the light, and was sitting with Brian while he tried to sleep.

Suddenly, Brian became very scared. He told his mother he could feel something touching his leg. Mrs. Dodd turned around and was horrified to see a huge creature creeping across the room. She described it as half-human, half-animal. She froze in terror as it came out of the darkness, and touched her leg too. Then it padded out of the room on all fours.

ROSS TO THE RESCUE

The two families were so scared by what had happened that they both moved out of their homes. The heads were sent to the home of Dr. Anne Ross, an expert in ancient peoples, to be examined. She thought the heads had been made by the Celts, a race of people who inhabited Europe thousands of years ago. The Celts often worshipped heads, which they considered sacred. They made many carvings of heads, and even cut off their enemies' heads and hung them up over doorframes. Dr. Ross wondered if the Hexham heads had been imbued with a Celtic curse.

This stone head, called the Hendy Head, is a good example of a Celtic carving. Could the Hexham heads be Celtic too?

THE BEAST IS BACK

Dr. Ross was a serious scientist, and the Hexham heads didn't scare her, even if they *were* cursed. She put them in a box in her study. But, a few nights later, she too had an eerie experience.

She woke up suddenly, feeling cold and frightened. Then, standing in her doorway, she saw the creature. It was half animal and half man ~ like a wolf above the waist, but with human legs. When Dr. Ross described it later, she said it was "covered with a kind of black, very dark fur", with a wolf's head. Dr. Ross was terrified, but felt a strange desire to run after the beast. She chased it down the stairs, but it suddenly disappeared, leaving her shaking with terror.

The monster that haunted the Dodds' and the Rosses' households seemed to have a wolf's head and upper body. It crept around menacingly, though it never hurt anyone.

The scary creature Dr. Ross saw resembled the werewolf, a monster which has featured in folklore and fairy tales for many years.

BRAVE BERENICE

A few days later, Dr. Ross's daughter Berenice was alone in the house when she too saw what she thought was a werewolf on the staircase. She was completely terrified but, just like her mother, she felt an irresistable urge to run after the creature. She chased it to the back of the house, but it vanished just as mysteriously as it had before.

The house was also plagued by banging sounds, footsteps and cold chills, and Dr. Ross's study door kept banging open and shut on its own.

CRAIGIE'S CLAIM

The story took an unexpected twist when, following national publicity about the case, a truck driver named Desmond Craigie claimed he had made the heads himself.

Craigie said he had lived in the Robsons' house in Hexham before they moved in. He had worked in a cement yard, and had shaped the heads out of cement one lunchtime. He had taken them home for his daughter, and they were eventually lost in the garden. The heads weren't Celtic at all ~ they weren't even old. But if this was the truth, how could they have gained their mysterious paranormal power?

QUARTZ QUESTIONS

The next scientist to study the heads had a new theory. Dr. Don Robins didn't believe in a Celtic curse. Instead, he showed that the heads contained a large amount of quartz ~ a mineral with a very regular microscopic structure.

Robins argued that this grid-like structure might be able to act like a computer, storing large amounts of information. This information might then be "played back" as a visual image, making people near the heads think they had seen a ghost.

Dr. Ross now felt sure that the scary events in her house were caused by a curse put on the heads by their Celtic creators. Not surprisingly, she decided to get rid of them, and had them sent away. As soon as she did, the haunting stopped.

SPOOKED SCIENTIST

Dr. Robins's theory has never been proved, although parapsychologists ~ those who study ghosts and other paranormal phenomena ~ are still investigating similar ideas.

Interestingly, however, Don Robins himself was scared of the two heads, especially the "girl". His scientific theory didn't make him feel safe at all. He said that, when he had the heads in his car, all the lights on the dashboard went out. And when he was at home, he felt the girl head looking at him, and was afraid to stay in the room with it.

Perhaps because no one wanted to keep them, the Hexham heads are now lost again. Who knows where they might turn up next?

This is a crystal of quartz, a common mineral. The Hexham heads both contained large amounts of quartz.

○ Silicon
○ Oxygen

Quartz has a regular structure, shown on the left, which Dr. Robins thought might be able to act like a computer chip and store information.

GHOSTLY JOURNEYS

PHANTOM HITCHHIKERS APPEAR IN MANY FILMS, URBAN MYTHS AND STORIES. BUT THESE APPARITIONS WERE WITNESSED BY REAL DRIVERS AND PASSENGERS IN CARS, TRAINS AND PLANES.

Most ghosts hang around haunted houses, creepy churches, or the battlefields where they died. But some ~ especially the ghosts of people involved in travel accidents ~ seem to haunt the routes of their last journeys. Often they hitch a ride with the living ~ only to disappear into thin air before their journey ends.

SILENT GUEST

This famous ghost story is from Stanbridge, England. On a foggy night in 1979, Roy Fulton was driving home from a darts match. He often gave lifts to hitchers, and when he stopped for a young man at the roadside he noticed nothing unusual. The man pointed straight ahead instead of speaking as he climbed in, but Roy just thought he was shy.

After driving along at 40 miles (60 km) per hour for a while, Roy decided to offer his passenger a cigarette. He turned to the passenger seat. The man was gone.

Gripped by panic, Roy checked the back of the car ~ but that was empty too. Somehow, the man had vanished ~ but Roy was sure there was no way he could have jumped out of the moving car without being noticed.

Roy Fulton picked up the mystery hitcher at Stanbridge.

WOMAN IN WHITE

In 1981, four friends were driving home to Montpellier, in the south of France, after a day at the beach. Up ahead, they saw a woman in a white raincoat. It was dark, so they stopped to offer her a lift.

The woman nodded silently and squeezed in between the two women in the back. The car set off again, and picked up speed. Then, as it rounded a corner, the woman shouted: "Watch the bend ~ you are risking your life!"

Startled by the warning, the driver slowed down and took the corner safely. But just then the two women in the back seat started to scream. Their mysterious hitchhiker had disappeared without a trace.

Montpellier

The French hiker was picked up here, at Palavas-les-Flots

MOTORCYCLE RIDER

When Corporal Dawie van Jaarsveld's hitchhiker vanished, he was more alarmed than scared ~ she had been on the back of his motorcycle. Worried she had fallen off and injured herself, he went back along the road near Uniondale, South Africa, where he had picked her up. There was no sign of her, and at last Jaarsveld went home.

But when he told his story to the police, he learned that he wasn't the only one to have had the same spooky experience. What's more, all the reports of disappearing hitchhikers on that route involved the same young woman Corporal Jaarsveld had seen. When investigators showed him photographs, he immediately recognized a girl named Maria Roux. She had died 10 years before at the age of 23 ~ in a car crash near the spot where he found her.

Corporal Dawie van Jaarsveld, photographed with the motorcycle he was riding when he gave Maria Roux's ghost a lift near Uniondale, South Africa.

GHOSTLY GIRL

Another accident victim seemed to haunt Maurice Goodenough as he drove along Bluebell Hill in Kent, England late one night in 1974. When a young girl suddenly appeared out of the dark in front of him, he had no time to stop the car. To his horror, he crashed right into her.

Maurice ran to help the girl, and found her lying by the road with a bleeding forehead. He wrapped her in a blanket from his car and, after failing to stop any passing motorists, set off himself for the nearest police station.

But when the police arrived, they found only the blanket ~ the little girl was gone. Even spookier, there were no bloodstains and no marks on the car, and police dogs could not find any scent to follow. They searched the area, but found no one ~ and no one was reported missing.

Goodenough left the girl lying injured beside the road ~ but when he returned she was gone.

SECOND SIGHTING

Almost 20 years later, in 1992, another driver, Ian Sharpe, had a very similar eerie encounter on the same road in Kent. But this time the girl disappeared before he even reached her side ~ although he was sure he had felt the bump as his car hit her.

Some say the girl was Susan Browne, who died in 1965 in a car crash at the foot of Bluebell Hill. But Susan was 22. Could Goodenough and Sharpe have seen a ghost of her as a child?

RAILWAY WIDOW

In 1900, a British soldier named Colonel Ewart claimed he saw a ghost on a train from London to Carlisle. At that time, trains were divided into separate compartments and had no corridors. When Ewart woke up from a nap to find a young woman in his compartment, he was puzzled ~ the train had not visited any stops, so there was no way she could have climbed in.

TRAIN TRAGEDY

The woman was dressed in black, and sat quietly, looking down with a sad expression.

Suddenly, the train jolted and a falling suitcase fell on the Colonel's head, knocking him out. When he came round, the woman had gone. But a porter he spoke to knew who she was.

Many years before, the same woman had been on the train with her husband when he leaned out of the window. Tragically, he hit his head on a bridge, and it was torn off and landed in his wife's lap. Now her grieving ghost haunted their compartment, constantly reliving her husband's gruesome death.

In old trains, there were no doors between the sections. The only way into a compartment was to climb in at a station.

FLIGHT 401

When an airliner crashed in the Florida Everglades in 1972, over a hundred people died ~ including the captain, Bob Loft, and the flight engineer, Don Repo. The crash was caused by a technical fault, and it soon seemed that the dead men wanted to make sure it never happened again.

This map shows the route of the doomed flight.

The two dead crew members began to appear on other flights ~ especially those that were using the same type of plane. Staff who had known the men swore they saw their ghosts ~ one woman saw Captain Loft's face watching her from an overhead locker.

On another occasion, a pale man in a flight engineer's uniform sat down next to a passenger, who then saw him disappear. She later recognized him from photos as Don Repo.

Repo's voice was also heard whispering to a pilot "There will never be another crash of an L-1011... we will not let it happen". Before one L-1011 flight, his ghost even warned the crew to watch out for fire on board ~ and he was right. The same plane had to make an emergency landing when its engines malfunctioned.

Don Repo, the engineer killed in the crash of Flight 401

SCREAMING SKULLS

THESE SPINE CHILLING STORIES TELL OF SKULLS THAT DIDN'T WANT TO BE BURIED AND PREFER TO STAY WHERE THEY ARE - FOLLOWING THE DYING WISHES OF THEIR LONG-DEAD OWNERS.

Can a dead person's head really decide where it wants to be? These four accounts from English country houses suggest that some skulls can.

BROOME'S LAST WISH

In a cupboard at Clifton Cantelo Manor in Somerset, England, sits a polished, shiny skull. It belonged to Theophilus Broome, who died in 1670. Most of Broome's body lies in the nearby churchyard ~ but before he died, he requested that his head should not be buried,  but should stay in his beloved home.

Not surprisingly, Broome's relatives were uneasy about having a severed head in their house, and at first they disobeyed his wishes. But when they tried to bury the head with its owner, something began to haunt their small village.

The story of what happened is told on Broome's tombstone. Moaning, groaning screaming, and other "horrid noises, portentive of sad displeasure" echoed around the village, and it was only when the skull had been dug up and replaced in its cupboard that the noises stopped.

STUBBORN SKULLS

Theophilius Broome has not been the only person to make such a strange request. A woman named Anne Griffith, who lived in Burton Agnes Hall in Humberside, England, asked for her skull to be kept in her house after she died in 1590. The skull screamed whenever it was removed from the house, until it was eventually bricked into the walls in 1900 to prevent any more trouble.

Even stranger is the tale of a skull kept in a house near Manchester. It is thought to have belonged to a Catholic priest who was executed in 1641, a time when there were many arguments between Protestants and Catholics in England. The priest's head was stuck on a church steeple, and was rescued by a Catholic family who took it to their home, Wardley Hall, to bury it.

But the skull refused to be put in the ground. Not only did it make strange noises if taken outside, it also mysteriously reappeared in the house however many times the family tried to bury it. Eventually, the family gave in, and gave the skull a permanent indoor home inside their house.

FAR FROM HOME

The most famous screaming skull of all is kept at Bettiscombe Manor in Dorset, England. In the 18th century the house belonged to a man named John Frederick Pinney. His family had made money in the West Indies, and when Pinney returned to Britain he brought an African slave with him as a servant.

The servant asked Pinney to have his body sent to Africa after he died. Pinney agreed, but unfortunately, he died first. When the servant also died no one bothered to carry out his request. Instead his body was buried in the churchyard.

Soon, eerie moaning was heard coming from the grave, and local farmers were plagued by storms, crop failures and disease. At last the servant's body was dug up and his skull was taken into the house in an attempt to end the haunting. This seemed to work, although it was said that the skull screamed loudly if anyone tried to take it out of the house. Even worse, anyone who tried to remove it ended up dead within a year.

Thunderstorms raged in the village of Bettiscombe when the servant's head was buried.

CHILLING CURSE

The curse was last triggered in around 1900, when a man stayed in Bettiscombe Manor and held a party. During the evening, he found the skull and threw it out of the house into a pond. The next day, the skull was no longer where it had landed. It was on the doorstep ~ up a flight of steps from the pond. No one knows how it got there.

In the 1930s, the manor's owner, Michael Pinney, was visited by three Australians. One of them said it was his father who had thrown the skull in the pond. He had died within a year, and his wife had always blamed the skull incident for his death.

The skull is still at Bettiscombe and has undergone several tests. One expert said it did not belong to a man, but to a woman who had died 3,000 years ago. Wherever it came from, its owners still keep it in the house rather than risk upsetting it again.

ANIMAL GHOSTS

FROM ANCIENT TIMES, PEOPLE HAVE BELIEVED IN GHOSTLY SPIRITS IN ANIMAL FORMS. COULD SUCH STORIES BE TRUE? THESE REAL-LIFE ACCOUNTS OF PHANTOM CATS, DOGS AND EVEN A MONGOOSE COULD HELP YOU MAKE UP YOUR MIND.

Animal ghosts can be just as frightening as human ghosts ~ or even scarier if they are large and fierce. Ghostly black dogs, werewolves and vampires that can take animal shapes have terrified people for centuries. But animal ghosts can also be helpful, like the ghost dog that appeared on a beach on the Isle of Wight (see page 82) to save two young girls from the approaching tide.

A ghost kitten appeared in this photo of a French boy whose kitten had recently died. The tiny ghost is on the left, nestling in the boy's hand.

FIERCELY LOYAL

Why would the ghosts of animals haunt the living? Several human ghosts seem to have been called back to this world by an emotional bond. For example, Lord Tyrone kept his pact to visit his sister after his death (see page 44) and the crew of a crashed plane returned to protect their colleagues (see page 77).

This kind of loyalty could also explain some animal ghosts ~ especially dogs, which often have a close relationship with their owners and are much missed after death.

In this photo of a tea party, a mysterious ghost dog is materializing. No one saw the dog at the time.

Witches and wizards were supposed to have talking owls as pets, or familiars.

TALL TALES

However, most animal ghost stories probably come from ancient folklore and fairy tales. For example, people used to say that the Devil could appear in the shape of a large dog, and that the full moon could turn people into werewolves ~ half-animal, half-human beasts who craved the taste of fresh blood and stole children to eat. Owls, bats, lizards and cats have all been associated with witches and demons.

The full moon was once thought to have magical powers, including turning human beings into evil werewolves.

BACK FOR REVENGE

Perhaps, like several human ghosts, some animal ghosts are seeking revenge for ill-treatment during their lifetimes. This could be the case with the Black Cat of Killakee (see page 84), which terrified the new occupants of a house where the cruel Earl of Rosse had once tortured and tormented helpless animals.

Our natural fear of wild animals could also help to explain how sightings of unusual, large or frightening-looking animals could gradually gain the status of ghost stories. But that doesn't mean to say that some of these eerie accounts aren't genuine hauntings...

In this old illustration, a witch rides an evil-looking black dog instead of a broomstick.

GHOST DOG TO THE RESCUE

WHEN A SMALL DOG, A LOYAL FAMILY PET, FAILED TO SAVE THE LIFE OF HIS OWNER, HIS GHOST APPARENTLY CAME BACK AFTER DEATH IN AN ATTEMPT TO SAVE OTHER LIVES INSTEAD.

This story begins over 60 years ago, when two girls from the Isle of Wight, in the British Isles, went to the beach to watch an ocean liner setting sail for America. Ryde, the town where they lived, has one of the flattest shorelines in the world. When the tide is out, the sea is ten minutes' walk away ~ but when it comes back in, it surges across the sands almost faster than a person can run.

The Isle of Wight, where the girls saw the mysterious ghost dog, is a small island off England's South coast.

COMPELLING SIGHT

The two girls gazed in amazement as the huge ship pulled out of port and made its way over to the horizon. It took some time to cross the bay, and as they stared, the girls paid little attention to the sea. They hardly noticed that the waves were beginning to wash up around their feet ~ until it was almost too late.

It wasn't until they heard a dog barking nearby that they came to their senses and turned around. To their horror, they realized that the tide was quickly cutting them off. They were standing on a sandbank, and a channel between them and the mainland was swiftly filling with deep water ~ leaving the girls with only a couple of minutes to escape.

PAWPRINT PUZZLE

The dog, which had white paws and one white ear, was standing at the water's edge yapping, as if begging the girls to follow it. Then one of them noticed something odd ~ the dog had left no pawprints in the sand. But she had no time to think about it as she and her friend waded to safety.

WALKING ON WATER

As they followed the dog, both girls saw something even more peculiar. Although they were wading through quite deep water, the dog seemed to float on top of the waves. And as soon as they were safe, the dog disappeared. When the girls told their friends what had happened, no one believed they had really seen a ghost dog. But one of their teachers had an explanation.

TIDE TRAGEDY

The teacher said that 40 years earlier, a tragedy had taken place on the same beach. Three young sisters and their pet dog had been playing on the sandbank when they were cut off by the tide. They had tried to wade back to the shore, the eldest girl carrying the youngest, Mary, who was five, on her shoulders.

But she tripped and fell, and Mary was swept away. Her little dog, desperate to rescue her, had paddled after her.

Neither of them was seen alive again. But when their bodies were swept up on the beach days later, the dog had still not given up. His teeth were clenching Mary's dress, and her arms were wrapped around him. What's more, Mary's dog had white paws and one white ear ~ just like the ghost dog who had saved the two girls.

The ghost dog had the same markings as the dog which had been swept away on the same beach 40 years earlier, while trying to rescue his owner.

THE BLACK CAT OF KILLAKEE

STRANGE NOISES, GHOSTLY VANDALISM, AND A MYSTERIOUS HUGE BLACK CAT TERRIFIED THE RESIDENTS OF KILLAKEE, A HAUNTED HOUSE WITH A GRIM AND MURDEROUS HISTORY.

Killakee House, near Dublin in Ireland, had stood empty for many years when Margaret O'Brien bought it in the 1960s. She planned to renovate the old building and turn it into an art gallery, to display the work of local artists and craftspeople.

When all the villagers warned her that Killakee House was haunted by a large black cat, Margaret wasn't worried. She knew gossip often gathered around old houses, and she decided the cat the locals had seen was probably just a stray.

VIOLENT PAST

There were certainly plenty of stories about the house. In the early 18th century, it had belonged to the Earl of Rosse, a cruel, violent young aristocrat. He ran a club called the Hellfire Club, which held wild, drunken parties at a hunting lodge on the hill behind Killakee House.

The Earl and his rowdy friends were known for their inhuman ways. At least three people were killed in duels at Killakee, and it was said that, at one Hellfire Club party, the young aristocrats beat an innocent man to death because he was a dwarf.

CAT CRUELTY

The Earl also hated cats and was known to have tortured them. On one occasion in Dublin, he soaked a black cat in alcohol, set it on fire and laughed cruelly as it tore shrieking through the streets, terrifying the local people. He and his friends also tormented and killed animals during their wild revelries at Killakee.

THE BEAST AT THE DOOR

After Margaret O'Brien had moved into the house, she did indeed often see a large, black animal disappearing into the undergrowth in the garden. It unnerved her ~ but she tried to ignore it. It was only when the renovations for the gallery began that she had to admit something more sinister was going on.

One evening in March 1968, three workmen were in the house, busy decorating the front hall. One of them, a local artist named Tom McAssey, had just closed and bolted the front door when it suddenly swung open, letting in a cold wind. Puzzled, Tom went to look outside.

This picture shows part of the long, low building which makes up the main part of Killakee House. In the background is the ruin of the hunting lodge where the Earl of Rosse and his friends indulged in wild parties and violent duels.

SPOOKY STRANGER

Standing just outside the door, he saw a strange figure, draped in a black cloak so that he could not see its face properly. He called out, "Come in, I can see you." In a deep, frightening voice, the creature replied "You can't see me. Keep this door open."

Tom McAssey's colleagues were so terrified they fled, and when the strange figure let out a deep snoring noise, Tom slammed the door and ran after them. But as he went, he turned and looked back, to see that the door had opened yet again. The figure had gone, and in its place crouched an enormous black cat, staring at him with red-flecked eyes.

The mysterious cloaked figure disappeared without revealing its identity ~ unless it somehow changed into the terrifying cat that Tom McAssey saw.

McAssey described the black cat of Killakee as "monstrous", and several other witnesses confirmed that the creature they had seen was much bigger than a normal cat ~ closer to the size of a large dog.

Oil paintings at Killakee house were torn and thrown around by a mysterious force.

RINGING OF BELLS

After the appearance of the giant cat, more strange things began to happen. One night, the sound of bells echoed through the house from dusk to dawn, even though the bells had all been removed from the front door and the bell tower long ago. There were strange banging and knocking noises ~ but even when the house was silent, anyone who stayed there overnight found it almost impossible to get to sleep.

One potter's works of art were found smashed to pieces in the new gallery.

ART ATTACK

Things got even worse when whatever was haunting Killakee House began to destroy valuable objects in the new gallery Margaret O'Brien was building. First, the workmen heard loud crashes, and rushed into the gallery to find furniture upturned and flung around the room. An antique oak chair had been smashed into tiny splinters. Another similar chair was not broken, but had been carefully taken apart, piece by piece. The nails that had held it together were laid out in neat rows.

Then the ghost turned its attention to the art exhibits. Paintings were dragged off the wall and ripped into shreds, and pottery was smashed and scattered all over the gallery. One potter seemed to have been singled out ~ every single one of his pots was destroyed.

The exorcism ceremony involves a candle, a Bible and a cross, which is thought to scare away ghosts and evil spirits.

ROMAN RITES

The haunting was so troublesome that, eventually, Margaret O'Brien asked a Roman Catholic priest to perform an exorcism ~ a religious ceremony which some people think can lay ghosts to rest.

This did seem to put a stop to the violent vandalism in the gallery, but the ghost still didn't go away completely. Instead it changed its ways and began to behave more weirdly than ever.

MILK MYSTERY

The first sign that the house might still be haunted came when Margaret went outside to get some milk. She had not yet bought a refrigerator for the house, and she had stored several bottles of milk in a shady stream that ran through the garden, to keep them cool.

When she saw that every one of the bottles had its foil top missing, she assumed a magpie had taken them. To protect the milk, she used stones to build a makeshift cupboard in the stream, with a slate on top to keep birds out. But to her amazement, the foil caps still disappeared each day, and were nowhere to be found...

The appearance of hats and caps after the disappearance of the milk "caps" seemed like a joke.

HAUNTED HATS

Shortly after the milk caps started to go missing, a different kind of cap began to appear. Dozens and dozens of different types of hats materialized inside Killakee House. They had not come from anywhere ~ they simply appeared, hanging on picture hooks and door handles, sitting on the work surfaces and lying around on the gallery floor.

This type of paranormal phenomena ~ something seeming to appear out of thin air ~ is very rare, and is known as an apport. Apports have sometimes been reported in poltergeist cases, but are hardly ever associated with ghosts. The hat apports at Killakee House have never been explained.

CHILLING DISCOVERY

The haunting continued quite harmlessly for a few more months, with more bizarre apports, knocking noises and occasional sightings of the enormous black cat. Then, in 1971, workmen dug up Margaret's kitchen floor to put in new plumbing. There, under the floorboards, they found a skeleton in a shallow grave a few feet under the ground. It had a full-sized head, but its body was unusually short. It was the skeleton of a dwarf.

Was this the same man who had been tortured and killed by the vicious Hellfire Club revellers? No one knows. But after the skeleton was given a proper burial, the haunting stopped. The house was sold again in 1977 and turned into a restaurant ~ and after that, the strange black cat of Killakee was never seen again.

THE MYSTERIOUS MONGOOSE

THE ISLE OF MAN IS NOT THE NATURAL HOME OF THE MONGOOSE, A FIERCE ASIAN AND AFRICAN ANIMAL BEST KNOWN FOR CATCHING SNAKES. WAS THE CREATURE THAT APPEARED IN THE IRVINGS' HOUSE REALLY AN ANIMAL'S GHOST - OR SOMETHING LESS SINISTER?

One of the weirdest of all ghost stories is said to have taken place on the Isle of Man, in the British Isles, in the 1930s. In some ways the strange entity that haunted the Irving family was like a poltergeist; in others it seemed more like a hoax.

Or was it really what it claimed to be ~ the ghost of a dead mongoose?

This map shows where the Isle of Man is.

The Irvings lived in a remote farmhouse called Cashen's Gap, near Dalby on the island's west coast.

SCRATCHING SOUNDS

The first sign of something strange came in September 1931, when the Irvings began to hear scratching, spitting and banging noises echoing around their lonely farmhouse. At first they thought there must be a rat or squirrel living in the walls, but they couldn't find it.

Over the next few days, though, both Mr. and Mrs. Irving and their teenage daughter, Voirrey, thought they glimpsed a small, unusual-looking animal in the house. It had yellow fur and was about the size of a weasel ~ but they never seemed to be able to catch sight of it for long.

Real mongooses, like this dwarf mongoose, live in Africa and Asia ~ not the British Isles!

COPYCAT

The strangest thing about the mysterious creature was that, even when it was out of sight, it imitated noises the family made. If Mr. Irving whistled or clicked his tongue, he would hear the animal do the same.

It also copied animal noises, and when Mr Irving tested it by singing a nursery rhyme, it copied that too ~ singing the song back to him, word for word, in a high, squeaky voice. The Irvings realized this was no ordinary pest.

Did Voirrey Irving, shown here with her dog Mona, fake the high, ghostly voice?

MONGOOSE MAYHEM

Once it had learned to speak, the creature told everyone its name ~ "Gef". Gef said he was the ghost of a mongoose, a type of small mammal, which had lived in India in the 1850s.

As Gef became more talkative, events in the house grew more and more peculiar, and the haunting began to resemble a poltergeist (see page 24). Dishes and pebbles flew through the air and the whole building shook with crashing sounds. One farmworker even saw a crust of bread rise into the air and float above the ground, just as if an invisible animal was carrying it.

DID VOIRREY DO IT?

At first Voirrey Irving seemed to be Gef's chosen target. Stones were thrown at her from nowhere, and Gef's voice was often heard insulting her. She was so afraid that she moved into her parents' room, but Gef screamed: "I'll follow her, wherever you move her!"

But Gef and Voirrey had so much in common that some people were sure she faked Gef. Like her, Gef loved talking about machines and technology. He also caught rabbits ~ and Voirrey was well-known for her rabbit-catching skills.

SOLE WITNESS

Voirrey was also the only person to see Gef clearly, and he only spoke when she was in the room. Could she have faked the high-pitched voice?

PRESS REPORTS

Gossip soon spread, and reporters and investigators arrived from as far away as London. One journalist who heard Gef's voice claimed that he saw Voirrey covering her mouth at the same time.

However, even if she did make the voice, the strange noises and moving objects, witnessed by several people, have not been explained. There have been many investigations and new theories, but the Isle of Man mongoose remains one of the classic unsolved ghost stories of all time.

In a mirror, a reporter saw Voirrey covering her mouth when the mongoose was speaking.

BLACK DOGS

LARGE, BLACK DOGS, OFTEN WITH GLOWING EYES, ARE THE MOST FREQUENTLY REPORTED PHANTOM ANIMALS. ARE THEY JUST A MYTH ~ OR DO THE MANY ACCOUNTS SUGGEST THERE IS SOME TRUTH TO THESE STORIES?

Ghostly "black dogs" are often said to have red eyes.

For hundreds of years, people all over the world have reported being haunted by the terrifying figure of a huge black dog. Sometimes the beast has glowing red eyes, or the power to burn its victims. Sometimes it is a sign of impending disaster or death ~ but in other cases it merely brings with it an indefinable feeling of evil. In some languages, even the phrase "black dog" has come to mean a sense of doom or depression.

THE BUNGAY BEAST

One of the best-known black dog stories comes from the town of Bungay, England. One stormy day in 1577, during a service at Bungay church, a huge black dog-like creature suddenly appeared in the church aisle. No one saw it arrive; it seemed to materialize before their eyes. It leaped on the parishioners, viciously mauled two of them to death, and disappeared. A third victim was left with mysterious burns.

The beast appeared at another church, in nearby Blythburgh, just a short time later. It ran through the church door, and left claw-shaped scorch marks ~ which are still there to this day ~ on the wooden floor.

FISHING FRIGHT

This black dog encounter was reported in 1928 by an Irish student who was fishing in a river in County Londonderry. As he sat on the riverbank, he noticed a dog paddling through the shallow water. At first he thought it was a normal dog, such as a labrador. But as it came menacingly closer, he began to realize that it was far bigger than any dog he had ever seen.

Suddenly filled with a strange feeling of terror, the student dropped his fishing gear and quickly climbed a nearby tree. The dog crept closer and closer, until it stood on the exact spot where he had been sitting. At that moment it turned its huge head and stared directly up at the trembling student, who was horrified to see that its eyes were glowing red, like burning hot coals.

The dog eventually walked away, and the witness would not come down from the tree until he had seen it disappear around a bend in the river.

The dog known as the Bungay Beast haunted two churches, one in Bungay and one in nearby Blythburgh.

Arielis erste Erscheinung.

This image of a demonic black dog known as Arielis comes from a German book printed in 1860.

DOG OF DEATH

According to legend, the Vaughn family, from Shropshirc in England, had their own phantom black dog, which haunted them for many generations. It always appeared just before a family member was about to die.

One descendant of the Vaughn family, who knew about the dog's scary appearances, decided not to reveal the family secret to his wife when he got married. He was worried that the legend would frighten her, and anyway he hoped that she might never have to see the creature.

A few years later, one of the Vaughns' children fell ill, and gradually got worse. One night, Mrs. Vaughn came running from the bedroom, begging her husband to get rid of a huge black dog, which had somehow found its way in and was sitting on the child's bed.

Mr. Vaughn's blood ran cold as he realized what the dog's appearance meant. He ran upstairs ~ although he knew in his heart that it was too late. His beloved child was dead, and the dog was gone.

GLOSSARY

apparition The word "apparition" simply means something that appears. A ghost that can be seen (rather than just felt or heard, for example) is an apparition.

apport An object that appears out of nowhere. Apports have been reported during poltergeist hauntings.

Celts A group of tribes who lived in various parts of Europe from about 2,000 years ago. Their religion involved worshipping carved stone heads.

crisis apparition A ghost of someone who is dying, or in great pain or danger, which appears to that person's relatives or friends (even though they may be far away).

curse A magic spell, usually attached to an object, which is intended to cause harm to anyone who owns it.

cyclical ghost A ghost that appears in the same place again and again.

demon A name for any type of evil spirit. Different cultures have different types of demons, but in many countries they are said to come from Hell and are the servants of the Devil.

Devil The most important evil spirit of all. In some religions the Devil is believed to be the guardian of Hell. He visits Earth to take people's souls there after they die.

Doppelganger This word is German for "double-walker" and means the ghost of someone who is still alive. Seeing your own Doppelganger is said to be very bad luck.

ectoplasm A white substance which, in the 19th and early 20th centuries, was believed to come out of a medium's body when he or she was in contact with the spirit world. It could come from the mouth, nose, ears or even the navel, and sometimes formed ghostly shapes. However, photos of ectoplasm show that it was probably faked using white cloth.

EMU or Environmental Monitoring Unit A tool used to measure temperature, air movements, sounds and so on in a haunted house or other haunted site. It records anything unusual and can be used to detect hoaxers.

ESP or Extra-Sensory Perception The ability to "see" or understand things without using any of the five senses (sight, hearing, touch, taste or smell). This is why ESP is sometimes called "sixth sense". For example, if you had ESP, you could tell which card someone had chosen from a pack, without seeing it or being told about it.

exorcism A religious ceremony which is sometimes used to try to drive ghosts or evil spirits away. It can involve lighting candles, praying and ringing bells.

focus In a poltergeist case, the ghost is usually attached to one person, who is known as the focus. Some experts think the focus may even cause the haunting.

folklore The traditional beliefs, superstitions and stories (including ghost stories) of a particular society.

ghost The image (or invisible presence) of a person or thing which is not really there ~ such as a dead person or animal, a sunken ship, or someone who is far away.

ghoul A type of ghost, especially an evil one. In some cultures, ghouls are said to feed on dead bodies.

hallucination An imagined vision. Hallucinations are not ghosts. They seem real to the person who is having them, but in fact they are illusions caused by the brain.

infrasound A deep sound, too low to be heard by human ears. It can make people feel uncomfortable, and experts think some "hauntings" are in fact caused by infrasound making a place feel spooky.

jinx A kind of curse attached to a person or a family, which causes them to have bad luck.

levitation Floating into the air as if by magic. Some psychics claim to be able to levitate, and some poltergeist victims say they have been levitated by an invisible force.

medium A person who claims to have the power to contact dead spirits and bring messages from them into the world of the living.

mirage An optical illusion, caused by light bending in the Earth's atmosphere, which can make an image of something appear far away from where that thing really is. Mirages may explain some stories of ghost ships.

paranormal "The paranormal" is a name given to events that are bizarre, unexplained or mysterious, or that seem impossible.

phantom Another word for a ghost.

PK or psychokinesis This word comes from the Greek for "mind-movement" and it means making things move just by thinking about them.

poltergeist A type of ghost, usually invisible, which throws objects around, makes noises and breaks things. The word "poltergeist" is German for "noisy ghost".

possession If someone is possessed, it means that a spirit or demon is occupying their body. The spirit may even speak out of the possessed person's mouth.

premonition A vision of something that is going to happen in the future. Many people claim to have had premonitions of well-known disasters, such as the sinking of the ocean liner the *Titanic* in 1912.

prophecy A prediction about what is going to happen in the future. For example, the ghost that visited Lord Lyttelton (see page 42) made a prophecy that he would be dead within three days.

psychic If you are psychic, it means you have paranormal abilities, such as being able to levitate, read minds or see into the future. The word "psychic" is also used to mean a person who is psychic.

quartz A mineral found in many parts of the world. Some experts think the structure of quartz may allow it to record information about past events. This could be an explanation for some types of hauntings.

RSPK or Recurrent Spontaneous Psychokinesis A type of psychokinesis (moving things using mind power) that is not done deliberately. Some experts think RSPK is what really causes poltergeists.

seance A session in which a group of people, usually including a medium, try to contact dead people's spirits.

soul The non-physical part of a person ~ their mind, emotions and personality. Some people think the soul dies when a person's body dies, but others believe that the soul goes to Heaven or to another world.

spirit This word is often used to mean the soul ~ especially a soul that has come back as a ghost. It can also mean any ghostly being with no body.

Spiritualism The religious belief that the spirits of people who have died can be contacted, usually with the help of a medium.

spook Another word for a ghost.

supernatural Anything magical or paranormal, which does not behave according to the existing laws of nature, is known as supernatural.

superstition A belief in something paranormal or magical. For example, a superstitious person might hang up garlic to scare away vampires.

telepathy The ability to send and receive messages using the power of the mind.

teleportation If something teleports, it disappears from one place and immediately appears in another. Books, clothes and other objects have been reported to teleport during poltergeist hauntings.

vampire A dead body which is thought to get up out of its grave and suck blood from animals and people.

werewolf A monster which is half wolf and half human.

witch A person who knows how to perform magic. Witches can be good or bad, male or female ~ but in many cultures the traditional witch is wicked, female and rides a broomstick. In the past, people were afraid of witches and anyone suspected of witchcraft could be tortured and executed.

INDEX

PICTURE CREDITS

Every effort has been made to trace the copyright holders of the material in this book. If any rights have been omitted, the publishers offer to rectify this in any subsequent editions following notification.

The publishers are grateful to the following organizations and individuals for their permission to reproduce the material on the following pages:

6-7 Photo of Glamis Castle: © Catriona Fraser (http://jump.to/catrionafraser), The Fraser Gallery, 1054 31st St NW, Washington, DC 20007. (202) 298-6450. FraserGallery@hotmail.com

9 Photo of knight reproduced by kind permission of Melissa Alaverdy. © Melissa Alaverdy.

10-11 Still from *Amityville II*: © Columbia-EMI, courtesy of Ronald Grant Archive. Photos of flies: © Digital Vision.

12 Photo of Borley Rectory: Fortean Picture Library.

14-15 Photo of Harry Price: Fortean Picture Library. Writing on wall: Fortean Picture Library.

16-17 Photos of Sarah Winchester and Winchester Mystery House: with thanks to Winchester Mystery House, 525 S. Winchester Bvd., San José, California 95128, U.S.A.

18-19 Photos of Treasurer's House and Treasurer's House cellar: Andreas Trottman/Fortean Picture Library.

22 Photo of seance ghost: Fortean Picture Library.

26-27 Engraving of Matthew Hopkins, Witchfinder General, and Engraving of Tedworth haunting: Fortean Picture Library.

29 Engraving of witch being tortured: Fortean Picture Library.

33 Engraving of monk: The Fotomas Index.

34-35 Engraving of witch and Devil: Fortean Picture Library. Illustration of witches in flight: Fortean Picture Library.

37 Illustration of witchburning: Fortean Picture Library.

39 Photo of Esther Cox's house: Mary Evans Picture Library.

40 Illustration of riverboat: Mary Evans Picture Library.

43 Painting of Lord Lyttelton and ghost: Mary Evans Picture Library.

50-51 Photo of computer: © Hewlett Packard. Photo of chemistry equipment: © Digital Vision.

52-53 Background water photo: © Digital Vision. Illustration of sea serpent: Fortean Picture Library.

54 Route map: © Digital Vision.

56 Photos of U-boat engine room, and U-boats at sea: Hulton Getty Picture Collection.

60-61 Photo of ghost at banquet: Fortean Picture Library. Photo of ghost on altar steps: K. F. Lord/Fortean Picture Library.
Photo of Greg Maxwell: Marina Jackson/Fortean Picture Library.

63 Photo of Loch Ness monster: A. N. Shiels/Fortean Picture Library.

64 Photo of lonely road: Hulton Getty Picture Collection.

66 Small photo of face in floor: Dr. Elmar R. Gruber/Fortean Picture Library.

68 Large photo of face in floor: Dr. Elmar R. Gruber/Fortean Picture Library.

70-71 Photo of Hexham heads replicas: Paul Screeton/Fortean Picture Library. Photo of Hendy Head: Mick Sharp Photography.

72 Illustration of werewolf: Fortean Picture Library.

75 Photo of Corporal Dawie van Jaarsveld: Fortean Picture Library.

77 Photo of Don Repo: UPI/Corbis

79 Photo of lightning: © Digital Vision.

80-81 Photo of boy holding kitten ghost, photo of ghost dog appearing at tea party, and illustration of witch riding dog: Fortean Picture Library.

82-83 Map of England: © Digital Vision. Photo of beach: © Digital Vision. Photo of dog: © Jane Burton.

89 Photo of Voirrey Irving and her dog: Mary Evans Picture Library.

91 Illustration of Arielis black dog: Fortean Picture Library.

First published in 1999 by Usborne Publishing Ltd, Usborne House, 83-85 Saffron Hill, London EC1N 8RT.

Copyright © Usborne Publishing Ltd, 1999. www.usborne.com

Printed in Spain
UE. First published in America in 2000